All Sorts of Science

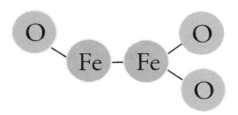

DOVER PUBLICATIONS, INC.
MINEOLA, NEW YORK

education.com

Bibliographical Note

All Sorts of Science, first published by Dover Publications, Inc., in 2015, contains pages from the following online workbooks published by Education.com: *Ode to the Olympics: Winter Edition, Hooray for Human Anatomy, Fascinating Facts About Earth Science*, and *Everyday Physics*.

International Standard Book Number

ISBN-13: 978-0-486-80273-2
ISBN-10: 0-486-80273-6

Manufactured in the United States by Courier Corporation
80273601   2015
www.doverpublications.com

CONTENTS

Ode to the Olympics: Winter Edition 1

Hooray for Human Anatomy 23

Fascinating Facts About Earth Science 47

Everyday Physics 73

Answers 99

ODE TO THE OLYMPICS:
WINTER EDITION

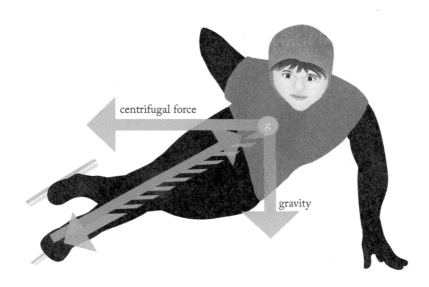

Winter Olympics
BIATHLON

Winter biathlon is a sport that combines cross-country skiing and **rifle shooting**. Biathletes ski around a cross-country trail broken up by two or four rounds of target shooting. During each round of target shooting, athletes face an additional challenge of having to slow their breathing and heart rate because they will have just completed a grueling segment of the race on skis. It's hard to hold a **rifle steady** when your heart is racing, your muscles are shaking, and you're gasping for breath! To make matters worse, athletes are required to hit circular targets that are only 45mm in diameter from a distance of 50 meters away, sometimes in weather that makes it **difficult to see**. The unique combination of skill, endurance, and mental focus required in the sport of biathlon help explain why it's the #1 televised winter sport in Europe.

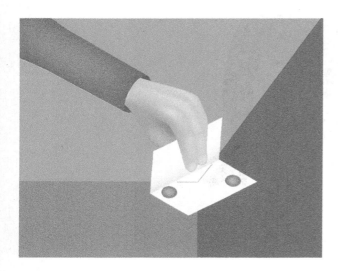

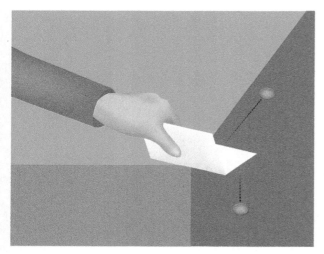

Try This!

Materials
- Table
- 2 coins
- Manila folder

Procedure

1. Cut the folder into a square of about 4 inches a side.

2. Fold the square to make a 2-inch wide flap. Position the flap so that it sticks straight up and down.

3. Place the square on the corner of the table with coins in the positions illustrated below. Grip the square firmly with whichever hand you'd prefer.

4. Now, give the manila folder square a sharp twist to launch one coin sideways while allowing the other to drop straight to the ground.

5. Listen for the sounds of the coins hitting the floor. What do you notice? Record your observations below:

_____

_____

_____

_____

_____

Winter Olympics
BIATHLON

Try This!

How accurate does a biathlete have to be in order to hit a 45mm target from 50m away?

Materials
- Plastic protractor with a swinging arm
- Laser pointer
- Pencil
- Paper
- Scissors
- Tape

Procedure

1. Cut out the targets below with a pair of scissors and set one up for target practice.

2. Fold along the dotted line to create a stand for your target. Stand your target upright on a flat surface outdoors.

3. Lie in the prone position like a biathlete would about 50 meters away from your target.

4. Place your protractor on the ground in front of you.

5. Tape your laser pointer to the swinging arm of the protractor. Make sure the laser pointer is lined up as straight as possible with the swinging arm.

6. Turn the laser pointer on, and move the edge of the swinging arm of the protractor so that it lines up with '0'.

7. Adjust the protractor so that the laser hits the middle of your target.

8. Slowly and carefully pivot the laser to the left or right. How many degrees can you pivot your laser before you're unable to hit the target? Read the result indicated by the protractor's arm. The number you record should be very small—biathletes have to have superb aim to hit these tiny targets!

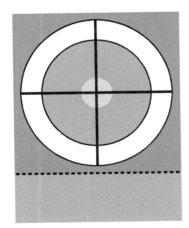 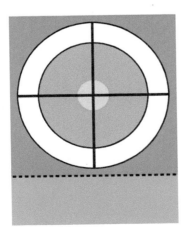 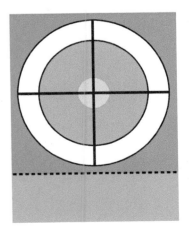

Winter Olympics
BOBSLED

What makes Olympic bobsledding different than just sledding down a hill on a snow day? You might be surprised by all the things bobsledders have to consider to speed past the finish line in the shortest time.

At the beginning of the race is the "pushoff." During the pushoff, bobsledders run as fast as they can while holding onto the sled for 50 meters before jumping inside. As the athletes are running, their feet are applying force to the track. This is an example of Newton's Third Law: when the athlete exerts a force on the track, the track exerts an equal force on the athlete in the opposite direction. The athletes train and build muscle so that they can create as much force as possible to push the sled forward during that 50 meters and achieve a high velocity throughout the race.

After the initial dash, the sledders get into the bobsled one-by-one, keeping it straight and steady so that they don't lose speed. At the 2010 Winter Olympics, the winning time for the four-man bobsled was 3 minutes, 24 seconds, and 46 hundredths of a second. Can you guess the times that earned silver and bronze medals? 3 minutes, 24 seconds, and 84 hundredths of a second, and 3 minutes, 24 seconds, and 85 hundredths of a second!

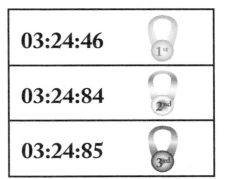

track exerting
opposite force on athlete

athlete's force exerted on track

Cool Fact: During a race, bobsledders are going so fast that they experience a force that's five times the force of gravity.

Winter Olympics
BOBSLED

For the rest of the race, the team works together to minimize drag due to air resistance, which will reduce their speed. They do this by keeping themselves tucked in as tightly as possible. The body of a bobsled is aerodynamic, which means that it's designed so that air flows over it smoothly. You can experience the force of air resistance by (safely!) sticking your hand out the window of a moving car. Even bobsledders' skin-tight suits are aerodynamic to help the team shave off those hundredths of a second to win the race.

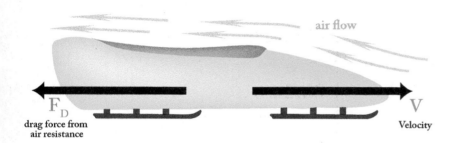

air flow

F_D
drag force from air resistance

V
Velocity

1. Sledders position themselves for the push off.

Starting line ---------------

2. The driver gets in first and retracts his pushing handle while preparing to begin steering the sled.

3. Then the pushers, who together apply the most force during the push-off, get in one at a time, also pulling in their handles.

4. The brakeman is the last to get in. He and the pushers tuck their heads in as low as possible to reduce drag on the sled.

Winter Olympics
BOBSLED

Try This!

Experiment with aerodynamics using a paper airplane made out of a sheet of 8.5 by 11 inch printer paper.

Think of the time when you're holding the airplane and winding up to send it sailing through the air as the push-off—for the plane to fly, the plane has to accelerate from rest just like the athletes must get the bobsled moving from rest at the starting line. Like the bobsledders during the push-off, you need to keep the motion of the plane straight and steady, or it'll crash right when you release it.

1. If the paper airplane is travelling fast and smoothly when you're holding it, it will continue to travel in the same way when you let it go. Practice throwing your airplane until you can get it to fly straight and steady several times in a row. Right now, your airplane is very aerodynamic.

2. Cut one-inch slits on each wing along the middle fold. Fold the two flaps upward so that they are at a 90-degree angle from the wing. Throw your modified plane several times.

How does the plane fly after you add the flaps? Does it fly as fast and far as before? Why?

_____

_____

3. If an object has more **mass**, it also has more **inertia**. So when a massive body is in motion, forces of friction have less of an effect on its velocity. For this reason, bobsled teams want to maximize the amount of weight in the bobsled. The weight limit in the four-man bobsled is 630 kg (including athletes and sled). If the team doesn't reach that weight, they are allowed to add metal weights to the sled.

Add a paperclip to the nose of your airplane along the base fold. How does it fly? Why?

_____

_____

_____

Winter Olympics
DOWNHILL SKIING

Downhill Skiing is less technical than slalom skiing. It involves fewer turns, but athletes ski at much higher speeds. Most courses exceed speeds of 81 mph, and the French athlete Johan Clarey broke the 100 mph barrier on a particularly fast course in 2013.

Check out the diagram illustrating the various forces acting on the downhill skier below. She has just triumphantly crossed the finish line, but she's still moving pretty fast! She now has to decelerate (slow down) until her momentum returns to zero. See how she's turned her skis perpendicular to the direction of her momentum? She does this so that she can exert force on the snow with her legs. The snow pushes back with an equal and opposite force, which slows her down. But to come to a complete stop, how much force would she have to exert on the snow, and for how long? Let's find out.

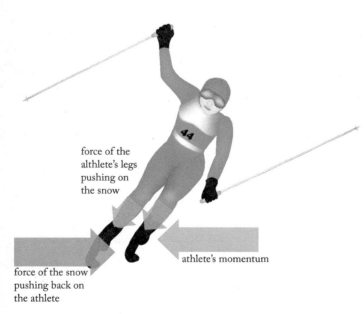

force of the althlete's legs pushing on the snow

force of the snow pushing back on the athlete

athlete's momentum

We'll pretend this particular athlete has a mass of 62 kilograms, and she crosses the finish line at a velocity of 28 meters per second. First, multiply mass and velocity together to get her momentum:

62 Kilograms x 28 m/s = _____ newton-seconds

The unit we use to measure momentum is newton-seconds. Newton-seconds tell us that the athlete's momentum really just comes from force measured in newtons (in this case, gravity) acting on her over a certain amount of **time**, measured in **seconds**. Gravity has given this athlete a momentum of 1736 newton-seconds, so we know that she'll need to exert the same amount of force back on the snow in order to stop: 1736 newtons (which is the same as **390 pounds**) if she wanted to come to a complete stop in one second. Crazy, right? Fortunately, skiers usually have more time to stop than that!

Try This!

How much force is in a newton? Think of it this way: weight is just a measure of how much force gravity exerts on something. There are just over four newtons to a pound. To lift a 5-pound dumbbell, you need to exert just over 22 newtons on it. Practice converting newtons to pounds using the following equation:

1 pound = 4.45 newtons

If a bowling ball weighs 2.2 pounds, it also weighs

_____ newtons.

If your bike weighs 30 pounds, it also weighs

_____ newtons.

If your textbook weighs 3 pounds, it also

weighs_____ newtons.

If you weigh _____ pounds, you also weigh

_____ newtons.

Winter Olympics
DOWNHILL SKIING

Try This!

Let's try to find out how much force each athlete would have to exert on the snow to come to a complete stop after crossing the finishing line.

Soo-ho, an athlete from the Republic of Korea, skis over the finish line at a speed of 32 meters per second. She weighs 62 kilograms. How much momentum does she have?

62 kilograms x 32 meters per second =

_____ newton-seconds

To find out the average force Soo-ho would have to exert on the snow to stop in three seconds, divide the above result by three:

Soo-ho would have to exert an average force

of_____ newtons on the snow to come to a complete stop in 3 seconds.

Sigmund, an athlete from Norway, skis over the finish line at a speed of 40 meters per second. He weighs 81 kilograms. How much momentum does he have?

81kg x 40m/s = _____ newton-seconds

To find out the average force Sigmund would have to exert on the snow to stop in three seconds, divide the above result by three:

Sigmund would have to exert an average force

of_____ newtons on the snow to come to a complete stop in 3 seconds.

Katja, an athlete from Germany, skis over the finish line at a speed of 35 meters per second. She weighs 64 kilograms. How much momentum does he have?

**64kg x 35m/s = _____
newton-seconds.**

To find out the average force Katja would have to exert on the snow to stop in three seconds, divide the above result by three:

Katja would have to exert an average force

of_____ newtons on the snow to come to a complete stop in 3 seconds.

Challenge: Divide each result by 4.45 to find out the average force in pounds each athlete would need to exert on the snow to come to a complete stop in 3 seconds. Skiers need strong legs with lots of endurance, and it isn't unusual for some of the top skiers to be able to leg press 800 lbs!

Winter Olympics
SLALOM SKIING

Newton's first law says that any moving object wants to continue moving in a straight line at a constant velocity (speed). The same is true of athletes on skis. But what happens during events like slalom skiing? Athletes have to complete many quick turns while remaining fast and stable. To do this, alpine skiers use their legs to push on the snow against the force of their own momentum—and the more momentum an athlete has, the harder she'll have to push. It isn't unusual for a skier to have to exert hundreds of pounds of force on the snow for several seconds in order to change direction.

So what is momentum, anyway? It's the product of mass (weight) and velocity (speed), and is represented by the following equation:

$$p = mv$$

Where:

- p = momentum

- m = mass

- v = velocity

If you're kind of stumped as to how this is all related, here's one way you can think about it. What's an easier thing to stop: a train moving at 30 miles per hour or a marble moving at 30 miles per hour? If you're a good catch, it's pretty easy to snatch the marble out of the air. But if you tried to grab a moving train, the train would just yank you right along with it! Why? The train has a lot more mass, meaning it has more momentum than the marble—even if their velocities are the same.

So what does this mean for skiers? A heavier skier may be able to accelerate faster, because his momentum helps him overcome forces like friction from the snow. Here's the problem, though—in order to turn or come to a full stop, he has to push a whole lot harder on the snow in order to fight against his own momentum!

Try This!

Have a look at the following pairs of moving objects. Which object **has the greater momentum?** To find out, multiply each object's mass and velocity and pick the larger number.

1. A 7 kg bowling ball traveling at 8 m/s or a 0.15 kg baseball traveling at 46 m/s

2. A 92 kg sprinter running at 9 m/s or a 63 kg cyclist on an 11 kg road bike traveling at 12 m/s

3. A 72 kg alpine snowboarder traveling at 21 m/s or a 61 kg skier traveling at 24 m/s

Winter Olympics
SLALOM SKIING

Check out the illustration above showing a slalom skier during various points of a turn. The red line represents the path that the skier travels in. But remember what Newton's second law says—objects don't naturally travel along curved paths! To complete a turn, a skier has to work hard to change the direction of his momentum (represented by the straight blue lines) by using his legs to exert a force against the snow with the edge of his skis. The force of the snow pushing back on the skis is represented by the green arrow. (This force has a special name. We'll talk about it more when we explore the physics behind speed skating!)

What else do you notice about the diagram above? Do you notice anything the athlete changes about his body positioning throughout the turn? Take note of his hands, torso, and knees. Why do you think he does this?

_____

_____

_____

_____

Winter Olympics
SNOWBOARDING

In the snowboard half-pipe event, snowboarders use velocity and torque to perform tricks in the air.

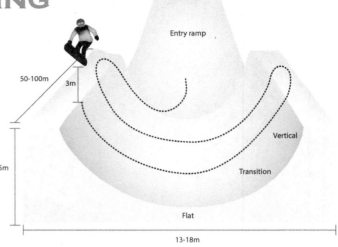

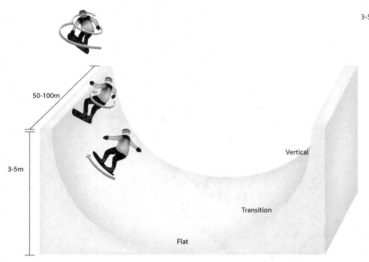

A snowboarder creates torque by twisting his torso at the "vertical" of the half-pipe. This turns linear momentum into angular momentum as he rotates around his own vertical axis.

Try This!

1. Stand up in a clear area. Make sure that you have enough space to reach out both your arms and not touch anything.

2. With your feet about shoulder-width apart, jump straight up. Do this a few times. What kind of momentum is your body experiencing? In what direction?

_____

3. You're going to jump again, only this time, twist by rotating your chest and shoulders left as you jump. What happened?

_____

_____

4. Explain how this happened using the terms **linear momentum**, **angular momentum**, **torque**, and **axis**.

_____

_____

_____

Winter Olympics
SNOWBOARDING

Before a snowboarder does a spin, he extends and "winds up" his arms. By doing this, he's increasing the length of his lever arm, making it easier for his body to rotate. Think about opening a revolving door—is it easier to open by pushing on the edge farthest from the hinge or closest to the hinge? When a snowboarder swings his arms, it increases torque, making it easier for the rest of his body to spin.

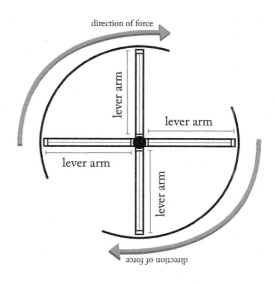

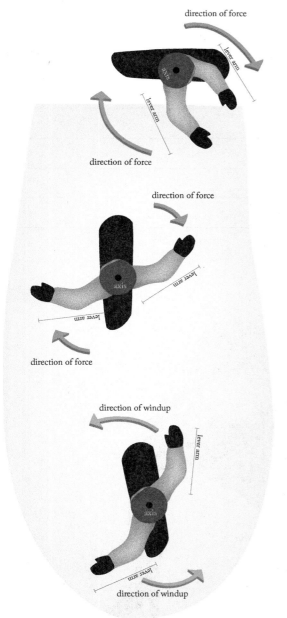

Stand in your original position. Without moving your feet, extend your arms away from your body. Point your right arm in front of you and your left arm behind. Your chest and shoulders should be rotated left. Now, as you jump, swing your arms clockwise. How did winding up your arms affect your spin?

_____

_____

_____

_____

Cool Fact:
If snowboarders maximize their torque on the half-pipe, they can spin up to 600° per second—that's nearly two full spins!

Winter Olympics
SHORT TRACK SPEED SKATING

In short track speed skating, competitors race each other around an oval track at speeds of up to 40 miles per hour. How do speed skaters lean so sharply during turns without falling over? The athlete pictured below isn't supporting any of his weight on his left hand at all! Remember when we looked at how skiers push on the snow to turn? The force that pushes back is called centripetal force because it causes an object to move along a curved path instead of a straight one. Speed skaters turn using this same force, exerted by pushing against the ice with their skates.

Centripetal force leads to an equal and opposite centrifugal force. Centrifugal force comes from inertia—the tendency of an already moving object to want to continue moving in a straight line. As the skater turns, he has to work hard to fight against this tendency. Check out the diagram below:

Need an example of how inertia works? Think about braking really hard in a moving car. Your torso gets "thrown" forward into the seat belt, but this feeling just comes from the fact that your torso wants to keep moving, even though the car is stopping!

Here, we can think of gravity and centrifugal force adding up to one big diagonal force (the dashed green arrow) that pulls on the athlete's center of gravity (g). As long as the athlete uses his skates to push back up through the ice with an equal and opposite force (the blue arrow), he'll remain perfectly balanced during the turn.

Imagine you're riding as a passenger in a car. When the car makes a really sharp turn, why do you feel like you get yanked in the opposite direction? Use the explanation of centrifugal force provided to help you come up with your answer.

_____

_____

_____

_____

_____

centrifugal force

g

gravity

Winter Olympics
SHORT TRACK SPEED SKATING

Try This!

Get a feel for how centripetal and centrifugal forces work! Remember: centripetal force is a push or pull that causes an object to move in a curved path, but because objects have inertia, they resist this pull (remember—moving objects prefer to move in straight lines). We call this resistance centrifugal force.

Procedure

1. Use your permanent marker to mark three evenly spaced points along the edge of your frisbee.

2. Using the hot glue gun, attach one end of each length of fishing line or string to each marked point on the frisbee.

3. Place the plastic cup on the center of the frisbee. Don't glue it down.

4. Tie the loose ends of each string together in a knot.

5. Add about 2 inches of water to the cup. You can add a drop of food coloring if you want—this will make it easier to observe the level of the water as you conduct your experiment.

6. Hold the knot you made in step 4 between your thumb and forefinger.

7. Swing the apparatus back and forth, slowly increasing the velocity after each swing. Have a friend observe the level of the water. What happens?

8. Try swinging the apparatus so that the string is parallel to the ground. Why doesn't the water spill out? What's responsible for holding the water in the bottom of the cup?

9. If you're feeling particularly confident, try swinging the apparatus around in a complete circle. If you do it right, the water shouldn't spill out! How come?

Materials
• Three 16" lengths of string or fishing line
• Frisbee
• Hot glue gun
• Plastic cup
• Water
• Food Coloring (optional)
• Permanent marker

Record your observations below, and try to explain the behavior you saw. How can you compare what you observed to how a speed skater keeps his balance during a turn?

_____

_____

_____

_____

_____

_____

Winter Olympics
ICE HOCKEY

In ice hockey, the slapshot is the fastest shot players can make, causing the puck to travel around 100 miles per hour! Let's take a look at the physics behind an effective slapshot.

Cool Fact: Most hockey sticks used professionally today are made out of aluminum, carbon graphite, and other materials that are stronger, more flexible, and lighter than wood.

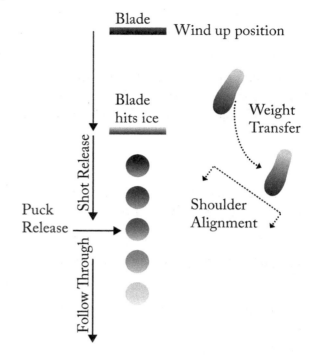

Blade — Wind up position

Blade hits ice

Shot Release

Puck Release

Follow Through

Weight Transfer

Shoulder Alignment

1. Player winds up the hockey stick.

2. Player "slaps" the ice behind the puck, flexing the stick.

3. As the hockey stick blade hits the puck, the player shifts her weight to her forward foot and rolls her wrists to transfer energy to the puck.

4. Puck leaves the blade, and the player follows through

Winter Olympics
ICE HOCKEY

Bending the stick against the ice is like compressing a spring. It packs the stick full of potential energy. Hockey sticks, like springs and rubber bands, are elastic objects, which means that they're flexible. When the hockey stick is in its usual position, which is straight, there's no stored energy. The hockey stick can be bent some without breaking (this is called deformation), but when it's bent, it will try to go back to its normal position. When the stick strikes the puck, that potential energy turns into kinetic energy, sending the puck speeding away.

Try This!

1. Get a plastic spoon that can bend about an inch backwards without breaking (biodegradable spoons tend to be more flexible than other plastic spoons).

2. Make a tight wad of paper about half an inch in diameter.

3. Hold the spoon from just the handle and load the wad onto the dip in spoon. Fling the spoon forward and observe how the wad travels through the air.

4. Now, do the same thing, only this time, pull back on the top of the spoon so that the handle bends. Release the spoon and observe how the wad travels through the air. How does this launch compare to the first? How can you explain this?

_____

_____

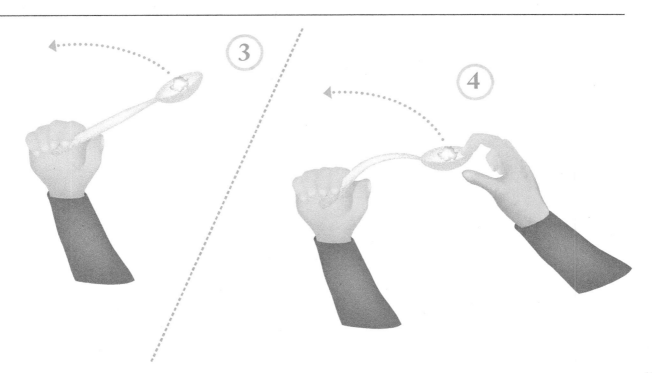

Winter Olympics
FIGURE SKATING

One of the figure skating moves that makes us "ooh" and "aah" is the spin, where the skater rotates in one spot at a dizzying speed. The skater starts the spin with her arms out, and when she tucks them into her body, she goes even faster.

This is due to the law of conservation of angular momentum. It's harder to make a mass rotate around an axis that's far away than it is to make a mass rotate around an axis that's close. When a skater tucks her arms in, their mass is closer to the axis, so it's easier to rotate—this is called decreasing the moment of inertia. Because angular momentum is conserved, her rotation speed must then increase.

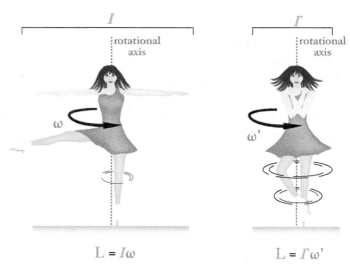

$$L = I\omega \qquad\qquad L = I'\omega'$$

L : angular momentum
I : moment of inertia
ω : angular velocity

Label the diagram for the variables:
L : angular momentum
I : moment of inertia
ω : angular velocity

Try This!

1. Set a swiveling chair in an open room, making sure that while sitting in the chair with your arms and legs extended, you won't hit anything.

2. Sit in the chair and begin spinning by pushing off the floor with your foot. Fully extend your arms outward. Keep kicking until you get a good spinning velocity going.

3. Pull in your arms, holding them tightly to your chest. What happens? Why?

_____

_____

_____

4. Extend your arms outward again. What happens now? Why?

_____

_____

_____

⟶ You can repeat the experiment with light weights in your hands, like dumbbells or books, to see an even greater effect!

Winter Olympics
VOCABULARY

Kinetic Energy – the energy an object has when it's in motion

Lever Arm (Moment Arm) – perpendicular distance from an axis to the line of direction in which the force is acting

Mass – a measurement of how much matter is in an object; mass can be determined by how much an object weighs—the more mass an object has, the more **inertia** it has

Moment of Inertia – a body's tendency to resist angular **acceleration**

Momentum – the product of the mass and velocity of an object

Newton – a unit for measuring force. One newton exerted for one second will accelerate 1 kilogram of mass by one meter per second

Newton's First Law – an object at rest stays at rest and an object in motion stays in motion with the same speed and in the same direction unless acted on by an unbalanced force

Newton's Third Law – for every action, there is an equal and opposite reaction

Angular Momentum (Angular Velocity) – the velocity of a mass in rotation

Linear Momentum (Linear Velocity) – the velocity, direction, and mass of an object

Potential Energy – the stored energy of an object

Torque – a force that causes an object to rotate

Velocity – equal to an object's speed and direction of motion

Acceleration – the rate at which velocity changes over time

Aerodynamic – having a shape or design that reduces **drag** from air

Angular Momentum (Angular Velocity) – the velocity of a mass in rotation

Axis – the line about which something rotates

Center of Gravity (Center of Mass) – the point at which the weight of an object seems to be concentrated

Conservation of Angular Momentum – angular momentum stays constant (if there is no **torque**)

Centripetal Force – a force that makes a body follow a curved path instead of a straight one

Centrifugal Force – a sensation that comes from an object's **inertia** resisting rotation

Deformation – the change in size or shape of an object due to a force

Drag (Air Resistance) – a force acted on a solid object in the direction of the flow of a fluid

Force – any influence that causes an object to change in some way

Friction – a force caused when two things slide against each other

Gravitational Acceleration – acceleration caused by gravity

Gravity – a force which tries to pull two objects toward each other

Inertia – the tendency of an object to resist changes in its motion, including direction; the more **mass** an object has, the more inertia it has

Great Job!

is an Education.com science superstar

Hooray for Human Anatomy

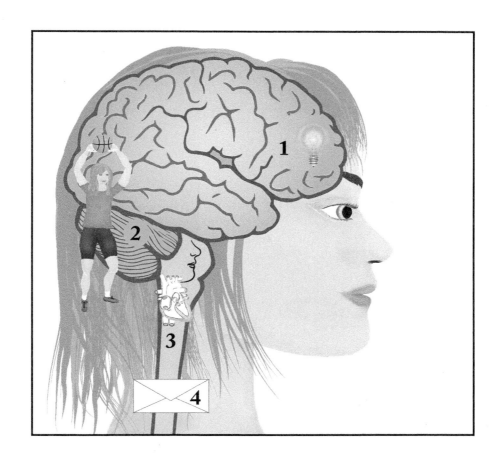

Color-by-Number Cell

The cell is the "building block of life." It is a basic structural, functional, and biological unit of all organisms.

Directions: Color in each part of the cell according to the color-by-number guide.

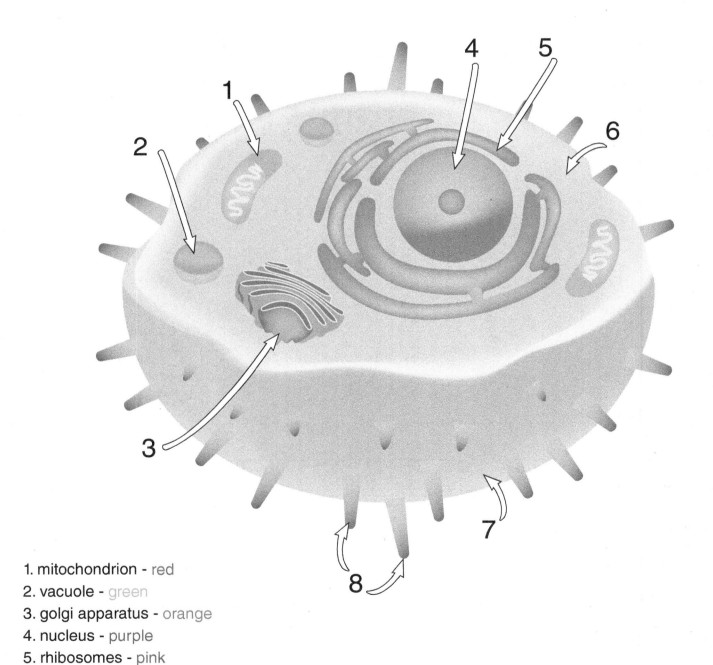

1. mitochondrion - red
2. vacuole - green
3. golgi apparatus - orange
4. nucleus - purple
5. rhibosomes - pink
6. cytoplasm - light blue
7. cell membrane - yellow
8. microvilli - light brown

Define Cell Parts

Directions: Have an adult help you use a computer to research these parts of a cell.
Write what each part of a cell does.

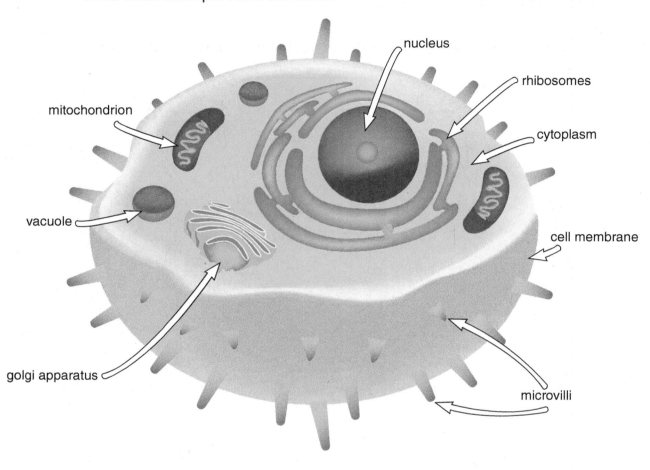

mitochondrion _____

vacuole _____

golgi apparatus _____

nucleus _____

rhibosomes _____

cytoplasm _____

cell membrane _____

microvilli _____

_____

How does blood flow through the heart?

Directions: Check out the diagram below that shows how blood circulates around the heart. Color in the veins and arteries the correct color to give yourself a better idea of what happens when your heart pumps blood.

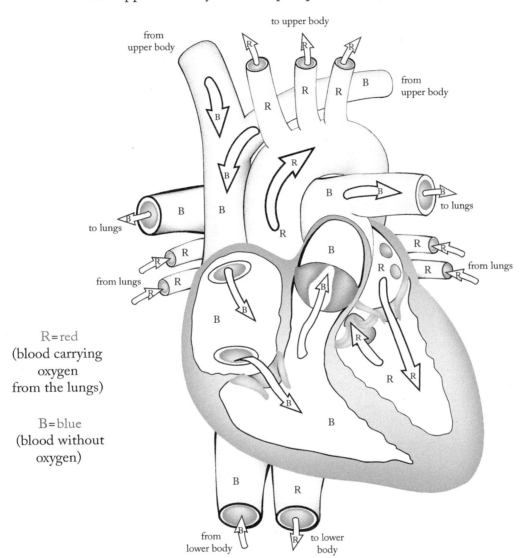

R=red
(blood carrying oxygen from the lungs)

B=blue
(blood without oxygen)

Extra Activity: Put your pointer finger and middle finger on the vein on the right side of your neck, right under your jaw bone. Find your pulse. Set a stop watch for 1 minute, and count how many times your heart beats. Write that number down. _____

Now, run in place for one minute. When you are done, find your pulse, set the stop watch for 1 minute, and count how many times your heart beats now.
Write that number down. _____

Was there a difference between the two times? _____

Why? _____

Brainiac

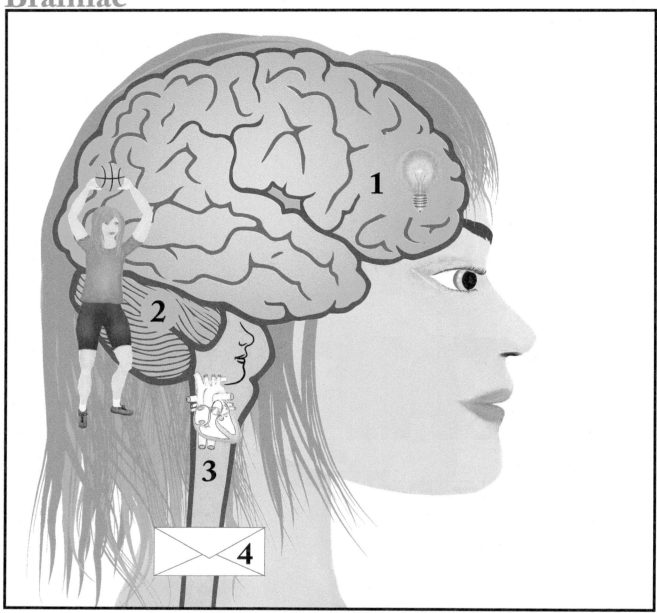

Directions: Use the clues in the picture to figure out what the different parts of the brain do. Match the part of the brain to the definition.

1. cerebrum   a. a bundle of nerves that sends messages to your brain

2. cerebellum   b. the thinking part of the brain

3. brain stem   c. controls balance, movement, and coordination

4. spinal cord   d. keeps you breathing, digesting food, and blood circulating

What happens when you eat?

Directions: Color in the different parts of the digestive system, cut them out, and glue them in the right place on the body. (hints: Start at the top. After the tongue, connect the pieces as you go. Glue the small intestines under the large intestines.)

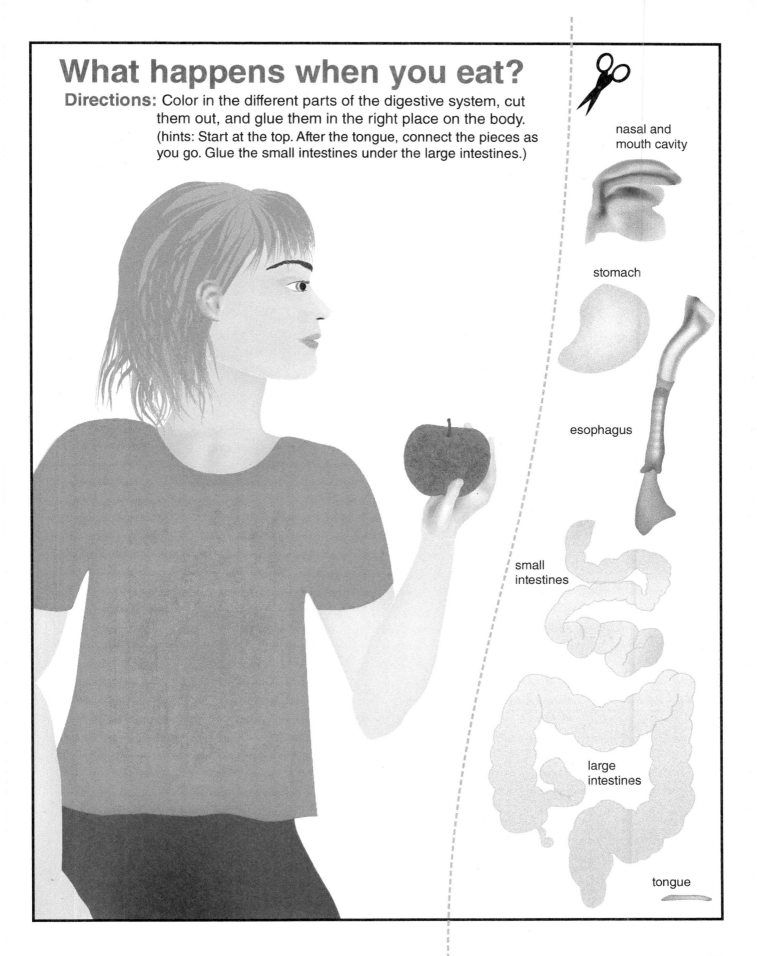

nasal and mouth cavity

stomach

esophagus

small intestines

large intestines

tongue

The Body's Filtration System: Kidneys and Intestines

Directions: Cut out each item from the bottom of the page. Each one describes a function of either the kidney or the intestines. Paste each one in the correct column.

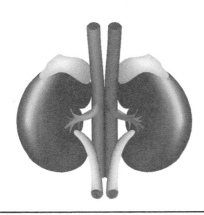
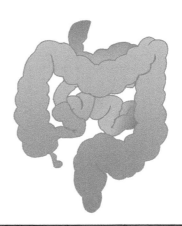

Pushes food through to the anus	Absorbs potassium	Absorbs nutrients
Regulates the body's pH balance	Cleans out the blood	Absorbs sodium
You can live with only one of these organs	Absorbs calcium	Lined with mucus
The waste from this organ turns into urine		Breaks down food

Your Respiratory System

Directions: Look at the diagram. Read about what each part of the respiratory system does. Label each part of the respiratory system on the diagram.

nose – contains two nostrils which brings air in and out of the body

answer: _____

trachea or windpipe – a tube that connects the upper respiratory system to the lungs

answer: _____

lungs – the main part of the respiratory system; it puts oxygen into the bloodstream

answer: _____

mouth – can be used to suck in or expel air

answer: _____

bronchi – smaller tubes that bring air to and from the lungs

answer: _____

diaphragm – muscle that moves up and down to help expand your lungs

answer: _____

1

2

3

4

5

6

(oxygen and carbon dioxide are exchanged in the alveoli, the small bulbs at the ends of the bronchi)

Where does the liver go?

The liver is made up of very dense cells. It's designed to filter the blood before it gets passed to the rest of the body. The main function is to detoxify the blood. It clears up chemicals the body can't take. The second function is to create proteins that help blood clot.

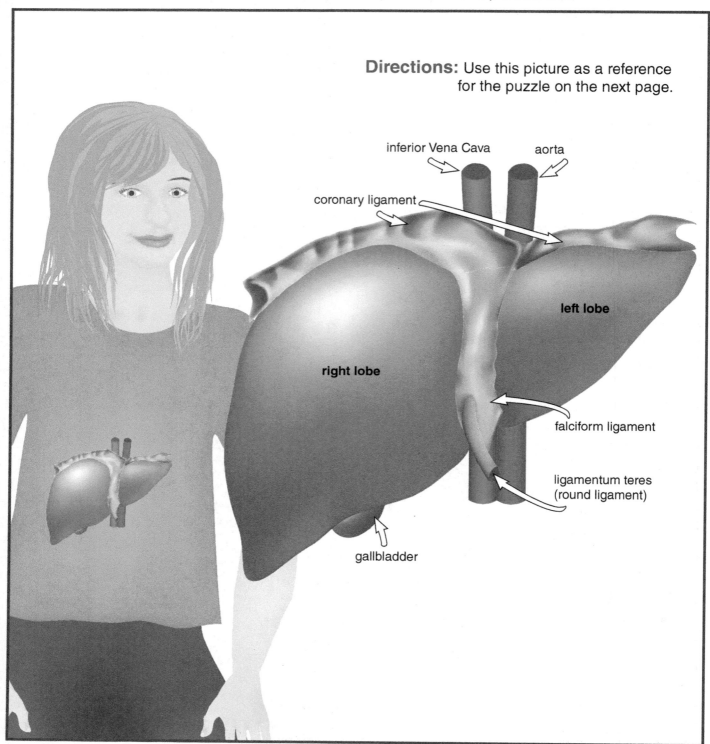

Directions: Use this picture as a reference for the puzzle on the next page.

inferior Vena Cava

aorta

coronary ligament

left lobe

right lobe

falciform ligament

ligamentum teres (round ligament)

gallbladder

Where does the liver go?

Directions: Cut out all the puzzle pieces below. Fit them together to discover all the different parts of the liver.

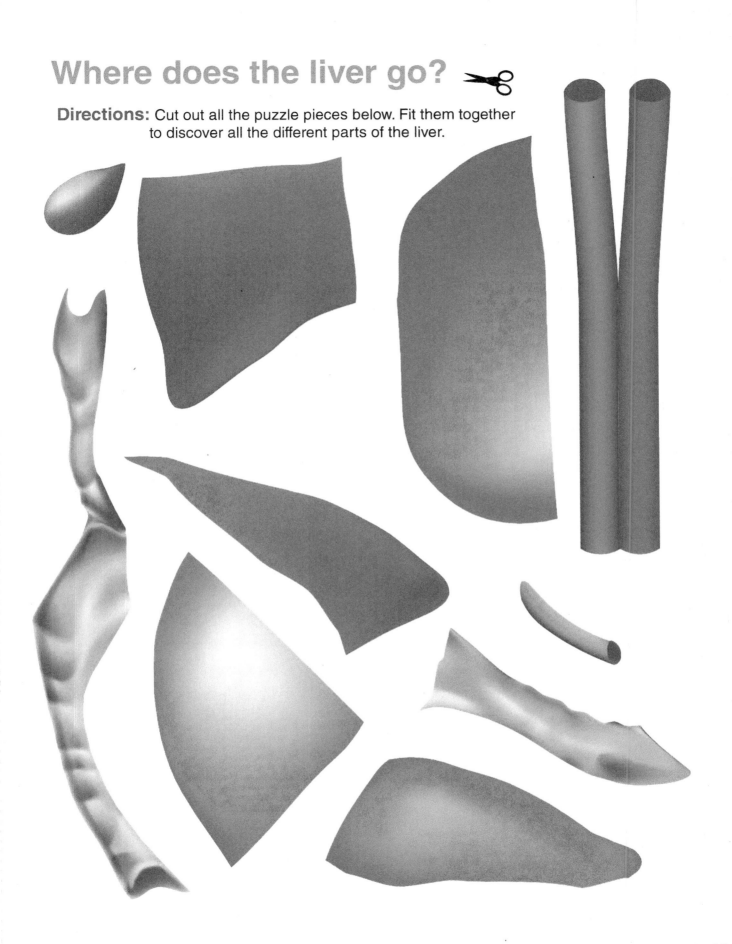

Are your lungs healthy?

Directions: Compare the healthy pair of lungs to the other types of lungs. How do you think each person's condition affects their ability to breathe?

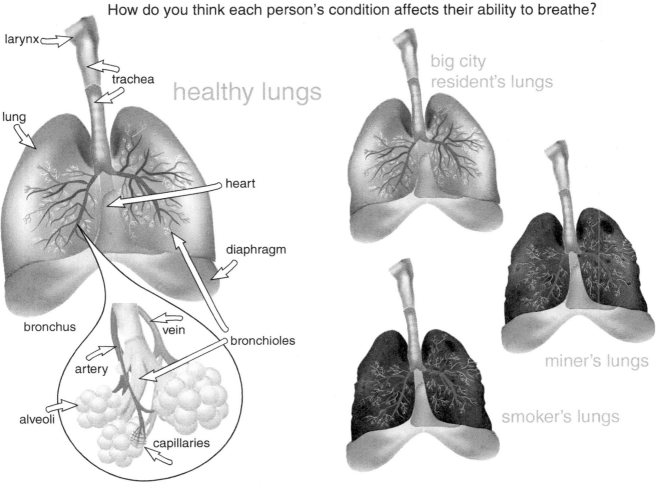

larynx
trachea
healthy lungs
lung
heart
diaphragm
bronchus
vein
bronchioles
artery
alveoli
capillaries

big city resident's lungs
miner's lungs
smoker's lungs

Word Scramble! Use the diagram above to unscramble these names of lung parts.

1. vielaol _____

2. gnul _____

3. terary _____

4. evin _____

5. tchraae _____

6. chusbron _____

7. brchionleos _____

8. rillapciesa _____

How many muscles do you have?

Answer: You have over 600 muscles in your body! A word search with all of them would be too big, but you can try this word search with 14 muscles.

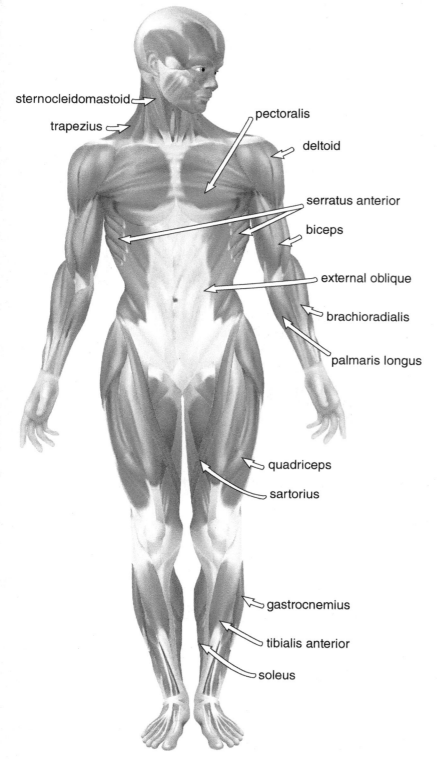

sternocleidomastoid

trapezius

pectoralis

deltoid

serratus anterior

biceps

external oblique

brachioradialis

palmaris longus

quadriceps

sartorius

gastrocnemius

tibialis anterior

soleus

```
S A R T O R I U S T O D A
D I Q J G V Z J E F H E K
Q V U M C X O P R S J L G
E D F G Z S D F R K D T P
X N B I C E P S A M N O B
T S D F L S E E T L W I P
E T L K D F S K U Q Z D M
R E L S O L E U S G D A P
N R G G F R H K A S K J A
A N S D H K F S N F I E L
L O S H D F S H T H E I M
O C A Q D H A S E W I N A
B L W Z U X N E R E Y U R
L E S Z D A J S I I Y U I
I I W Y F X D M O L E V S
Q D X M K L R R R F L G L
U O X M N C U R I P A E O
E M X C S H J W A C F G N
Z A X C T P L J I N E H G
Y S K N I V C O W V E P U
V T S H B F H S E C K B S
X O A S I J F H E U C O N
Z I C N A E S H F E H L B
O D S D L J E H U H J C R
E I U C I H W E J Z C X A
Z M K S S E U D J K S D C
M N C J A H E U E Y C J H
Z M X C N N D E E H U D I
W P E C T O R A L I S K O
A K S D E R D F I U J X R
Z N C H R H A U S H J C A
O L K S I E H P N C K D D
A M Z N O H D Y E G R U I
K S N C R Z M X N Z H E A
M Z N X H B C K S W I P L
M N Q O E D Y U F O H U I
G A S T R O C N E M I U S
```

What does the pancreas do?

Directions: Study the picture, and read the information below.
Use the facts to fill in the paragraph below about your pancreas.

The endocrine system is a network of glands that release different hormones to regulate the body.

The pancreas is a very unique organ. It is actually a part of two systems, as it does two jobs. The main function is to create hormones like insulin and glucagon.

It also creates digestive enzymes that break down carbohydrates and proteins from foods on the way to the small intestine.

tail

body

pancreatic duct

head

The pancreas is part of the

_____ system.

There are four main parts of the pancreas:

_____,

_____,

_____,

and _____.

The pancreas has _____ jobs.

The main job of the pancreas is to release

_____ to regulate the body.

The other job is to create _____

that break down carbohydrates and proteins from foods.

The pancreas is a very important part of your body.

Your Body

Directions: Trace the outline of your body on a large piece of white butcher paper, or tape several pieces of white printer paper together. Lie down on the paper, with your head turned to one side, and have a friend or parent trace your body. Use the diagrams of the systems on the following pages to help you draw detailed pictures of all the systems on your body outline. Label each system on your body.

Suggestion: Some of the systems overlap each other. Draw the first system on the butcher paper, then take a piece of white paper, and tape the left side only down to the butcher paper. Now, you can draw the second system. It's like a flap book where you can pull up the paper and see the system underneath.

Brain

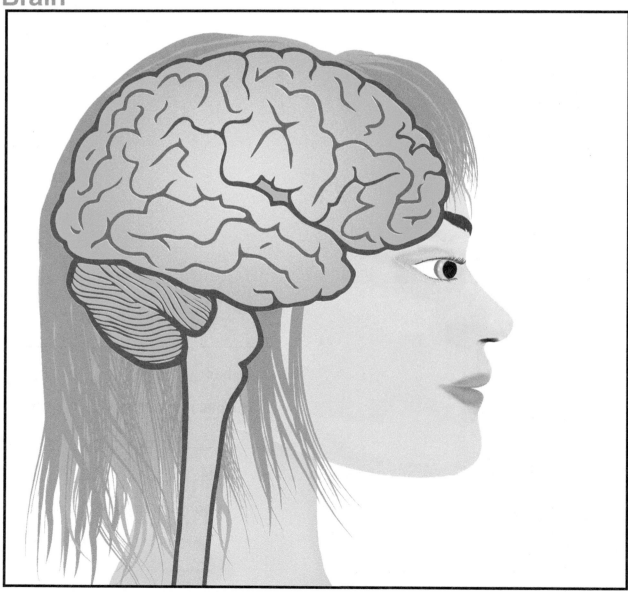

Your Body

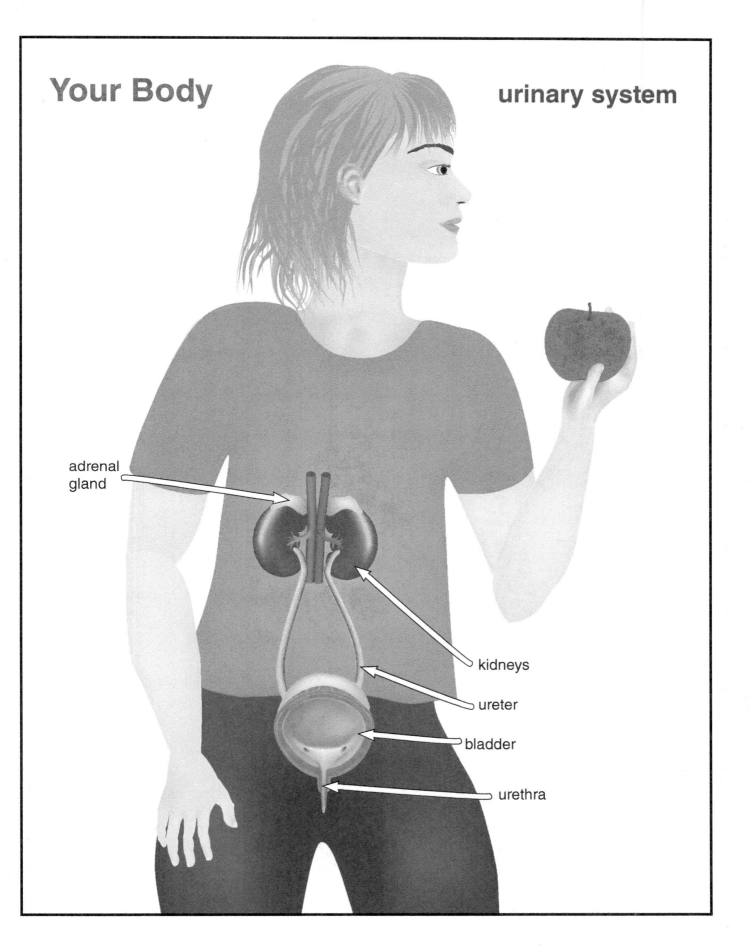

adrenal gland

kidneys

ureter

bladder

urethra

Your Body

digestive system

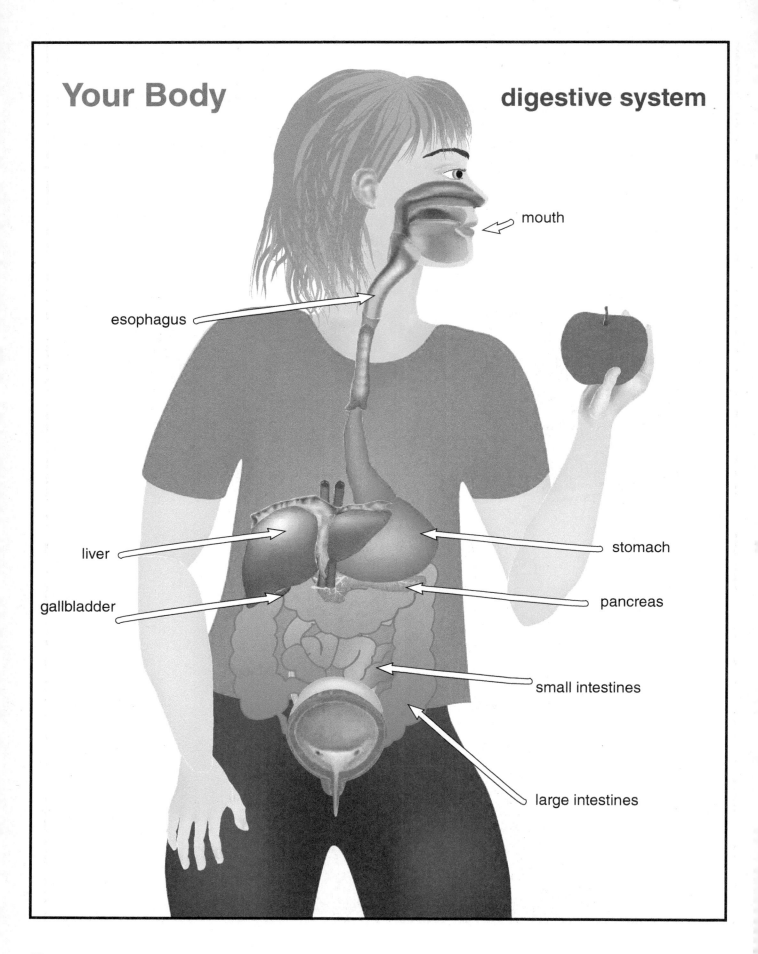

mouth

esophagus

liver

gallbladder

stomach

pancreas

small intestines

large intestines

Your Body

respiratory system

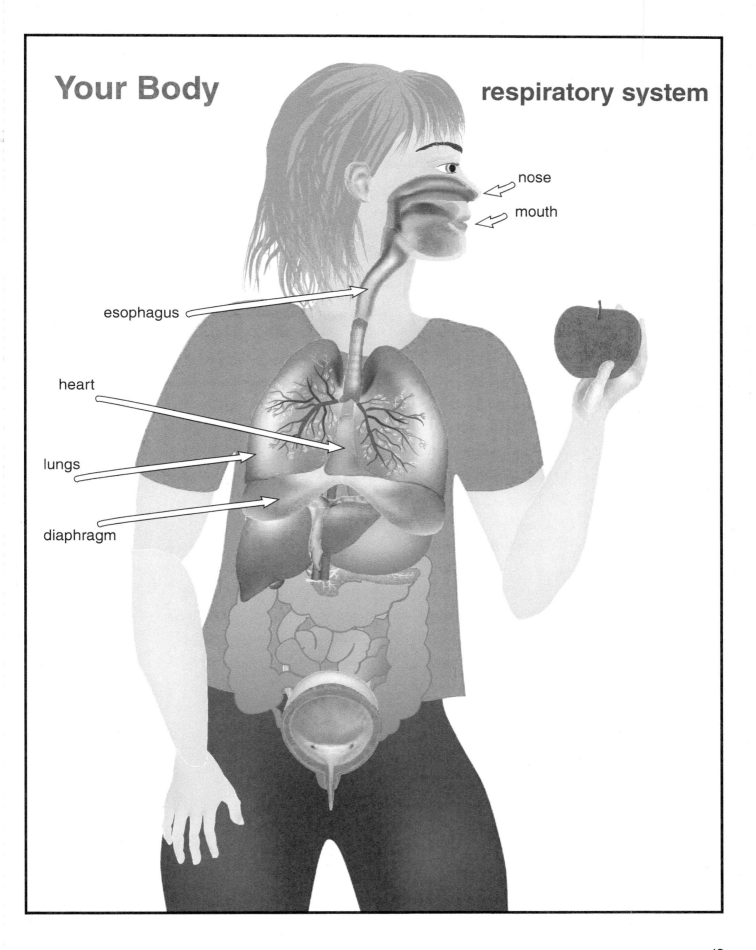

nose

mouth

esophagus

heart

lungs

diaphragm

Great job!

is an Education.com science superstar

FASCINATING FACTS
ABOUT EARTH SCIENCE

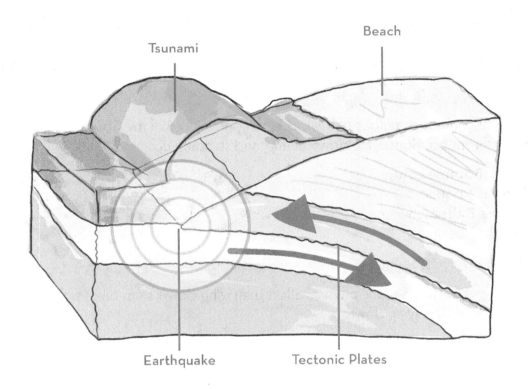

Tsunami

Beach

Earthquake

Tectonic Plates

Scientist Dr. E. McSquare is compiling his scientific findings into a single volume. He forgot to give titles to the sections of his reports and now they're all mixed up! Use the definition guide to help Dr. McSquare label his reports.

Definition Guide:

Q = Question: The question is the first part of the scientific process. What question do you want to answer?

H = Hypothesis: A hypothesis is a statement that can be proven true or false. It is often written in the form "If (a) then (b)."

E = Experiment: The experiment is an activity that is used to test if your hypothesis is true or false.

D = Data: Data are the results of the experiment.

C = Conclusion: The conclusion is a final statement that describes what you learned from the experiment and results.

___**E**___ I will count count the number of heart beats in one minute of my laboratory partners in three different positions: lying down, sitting, and standing up.

_____ **Object: Bounce count**
Golf ball: 4 bounces
Medicine Ball: 7 bounces
Baseball: 5 bounces

_____ Do heavier objects bounce higher on a trampoline?

_____ If standing up requires more physical effort than lying down, then one's pulse standing up will be greater than lying down.

_____ From a fixed height, I will drop a variety of objects onto a trampoline several times and observe the number of bounces before the object stops bouncing assuming objects that bounce higher will bounce the most number of times.

_____ If there is an equal and opposite reaction to every action, then heavier objects will bounce higher off a trampoline.

_____ **Maurice:** Lying down - 55 bpm, **Sitting** - 59 bpm, **Standing** - 65 bpm
Lucy: Lying down - 58 bpm, **Sitting** - 60 bpm, **Standing** - 70 bpm
Carlos: Lying down - 51 bpm, **Sitting** - 54 bpm, **Standing** - 56 bpm

_____ How does one's pulse change in different physical positions?

_____ The experiment and data show that heavier objects bounce higher on trampolines.

_____ A person's stationary position affects his or her heart rate. The heart rate is higher if the upper body is upright.

Scientist Dr. E. McSquare is compiling his scientific findings into a single volume. He forgot to give titles to the sections of his reports and now they're all mixed up! Use the definition guide to help Dr. McSquare label his reports.

Definition Guide:

Q = Question: The question is the first part of the scientific process. What question do you want to answer?

H = Hypothesis: A hypothesis is a statement that can be proven true or false. It is often written in the form "If (a) then (b)."

E = Experiment: The experiment is an activity that is used to test if your hypothesis is true or false.

D = Data: Data are the results of the experiment.

C = Conclusion: The conclusion is a final statement that describes what you learned from the experiment and results.

_C_ The results of this experiment show that the boiling point of water does rise as the amount of salt in the water increases.

_____ I will drop a variety of objects from a height of 10 feet and use a stopwatch to record the time it takes for them to hit the ground.

_____ Ignoring wind resistance, if two objects are dropped at the same time, they will both hit the ground at the same time because gravity is the same for both of them.

_____ The results of this experiment showed that objects fall at the same rate despite weight differences.

_____ **Object (weight) (drop time)**
Shoe: (15 oz) (.82 seconds)
Bowling ball: (12 pounds) (.82 seconds)
Pencil: (2 oz) (.84 seconds)

_____ I will put a thermometer in each of 3 pots of boiling water. Each pot will contain a different amount of salt. I will observe and compare the temperatures in each pot when the water begins to boil.

_____ Does adding salt change the temperature at which water begins to boil?

_____ Do heavier objects fall faster than lighter objects?

_____ **Temperature when boiling begins (salt quantity)**
Pot 1: 214.2 F (0g)
Pot 2: 216.3 F (50g)
Pot 3: 218.3 F (100g)

_____ If adding salt to water increases the density of water, then it requires more energy to make it boil, thus increasing the boiling point temperature.

Scientist Dr. E. McSquare is compiling his scientific findings into a single volume. He forgot to give titles to the sections of his reports and now they're all mixed up! Use the definition guide to help Dr. McSquare label his reports.

Definition Guide:

Q = Question: The question is the first part of the scientific process. What question do you want to answer?

H = Hypothesis: A hypothesis is a statement that can be proven true or false. It is often written in the form "If (a) then (b)."

E = Experiment: The experiment is an activity that is used to test if your hypothesis is true or false.

D = Data: Data are the results of the experiment.

C = Conclusion: The conclusion is a final statement that describes what you learned from the experiment and results.

___H___ If plants reflect green light, then they must absorb red light (the opposite of green) and thus grow more under red lights.

_____ **Plant Specimen - Light color: Growth**
Yellow Hibiscus - Green light: +9.4cm, **Red light:** +12.2cm, **Blue light:** 11.9cm
Golden Sage - Green light: +6.6cm, **Red light:** +8.1cm, **Blue light:** +7.1cm
Soybean Plant - Green light: +7.4cm, **Red light:** +10.1cm, **Blue light:** +10.0cm
Common Gardenia - Green light: +5.1cm, **Red light:** +6.9cm, **Blue light:** +6.9cm

_____ I will place 4 different plant specimens under green lights and compare their growth over the period of a month with identical plants under red and blue lights.

_____ Using clear containers with measurement marks, I will compare the height of water at room and freezing temperatures.

_____ Which color lights cause plants to grow more effectively?

_____ **Container# - State of water: height**
Container 1 - Water: 14.0ml, ice: 14.8ml
Container 2 - Water: 20.0ml, ice: 20.8ml
Container 3 - Water: 24.0ml, ice: 24.9ml

_____ Does water change volume when it freezes?

_____ After consistent results, water, when frozen, increases in volume in comparison to its liquid form.

_____ The results of this experiment showed that green light was the least effective color for growing our plants. Blue and red lights caused for the greatest amount of growth to occur.

_____ If the molecular structure of solids is more dense than liquids, then water will decrease in volume when it freezes.

Scientist Dr. E. McSquare is compiling his scientific findings into a single volume. He forgot to give titles to the sections of his reports and now they're all mixed up! Use the definition guide to help Dr. McSquare label his reports.

Definition Guide:

Q = Question: The question is the first part of the scientific process. What question do you want to answer?

H = Hypothesis: A hypothesis is a statement that can be proven true or false. It is often written in the form "If (a) then (b)."

E = Experiment: The experiment is an activity that is used to test if your hypothesis is true or false.

D = Data: Data are the results of the experiment.

C = Conclusion: The conclusion is a final statement that describes what you learned from the experiment and results.

___**Q**___ Do snails crawl faster on concrete or glass?

_____ **Amber: Left eye:** decreased. **Right eye:** decreased.
Julio: Left eye: decreased. **Right eye:** decreased.
Claudia: Left eye: decreased. **Right eye:** decreased.

_____ With my laboratory partners, I will cover one eye and shine a light directly into the other. Then, I will categorize the change in pupil size as "increased," "decreased," or "no change."

_____ If snails move faster on smoother surfaces, then a snail will move faster on glass than on concrete.

_____ The results of the experiment showed that pupil size decreases when there is more light present. This is likely due to the stress direct light causes on the eyes. In order to absorb less light, the pupils shrink.

_____ **Snail 1:** Glass - 45s, Concrete - 55s
Snail 2: Glass - 49s, Concrete - 49s
Snail 3: Glass - 55s, Concrete - 56s

_____ If a pupil detects the amount of light that is visible, then it will decrease in size when there is more light in order to take in less light and reduce straining the eye.

_____ Snails move faster on glass than on concrete.

_____ What makes the pupil in the eye dilate?

_____ I will organize snail races on glass and concrete and compare times of each snail between the surfaces.

Hydrogen

Hydrogen is the most common element in the universe. In fact, about 75% of the mass of the universe is made of hydrogen atoms! Hydrogen is the first element on the periodic table and got its name because it is found in water (Hydro means water in Latin). Scientists use the capital letter H to represent Hydrogen.

The chemical formula for water is H_2O. This means there are two hydrogen atoms and one oxygen atom in each water molecule. Look at the chemical formulas below and write how many hydrogen atoms are in each one.

water H_2O _____

Space ships use hydrogen and oxygen as fuel; the byproduct of the explosion is water.

methane CH_4 _____

Methane is a byproduct of decomposing organic matter; it is used as a fuel at some landfills.

glucose $C_6H_{12}O_6$ _____

Glucose is the sugar plants use as food, and is produced through photosynthesis.

ammonia NH_3 _____

Ammonia is often used in fertilizers because of its nitrogen content, which is essential for most plants.

caffeine $C_8H_{10}N_4O_2$ _____

Caffeine is found in many plant leaves; it is a natural insecticide because it often kills insects when they ingest it.

vitamin C $C_6H_8O_6$ _____

Vitamin C is important for nearly all animals. Humans are one of only a few species that do not produce it and must get it from food with large amounts of the vitamin.

baking soda $NaHCO_3$ _____

Baking soda is used in the body to neutralize some of the acids produced by the stomach.

The Water Cycle

Since the beginning of Earth, no water has ever been added to or taken from our atmosphere. It is constantly moving in a water cycle. Read the definitions below and put the corresponding letter in the squares marking each part of the water cycle in the diagram.

A Evaporation:
Liquid water is heated by the sun until it rises as water vapor into the atmosphere.

B Precipitation:
Water falling to the Earth in the form of weather - including rain, sleet, hail and snow.

C Condensation:
Water vapor molecules join together, becoming liquid, in the form of clouds.

D The Sun:
Creates all of the weather on Earth through the uneven heating of Earth's surface.

E Liquid Water:
All living things need this to survive and it is an important part of the weather system.

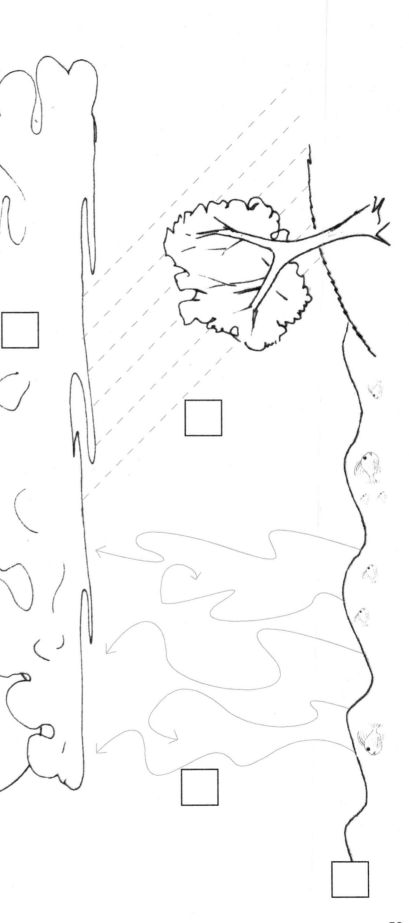

Photosynthesis

Use the word bank below to fill in the empty spaces in the paragraph to the right.

WORD BANK

CARBON DIOXIDE
CHLOROPHYLL
GLUCOSE
FOOD
LIGHT
BREATHING
WATER

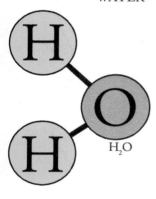

H_2O

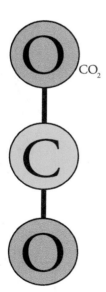

CO_2

Photosynthesis is a process where plants create their own _____ using sunlight.

Plant leaves absorb red and blue _____ into their leaves, reflecting green light. This is why most plants are green in color. A chemical called _____ is found inside most plant cells. This is the substance that absorbs sunlight.

Meanwhile, plants are absorbing _____ (H_2O) through their roots and storing it within their cells. When the sunlight hits the water molecules, the water breaks apart into hydrogen and oxygen.

Plants also take _____ (CO_2) in through holes in their leaves, called stomata. This is a plant's way of _____. When the carbon dioxide combines with hydrogen, a type of sugar called _____ is formed. This is a plant's food, and it uses this energy to live and grow. The extra oxygen molecules are released back into the atmosphere.

The Sun

The sun is our star. All of the planets in our solar system orbit around it. It is made of very hot gases, mostly hydrogen and helium, that provide the light and heat for our solar system. Answer the questions at the bottom of the page using what you have learned.

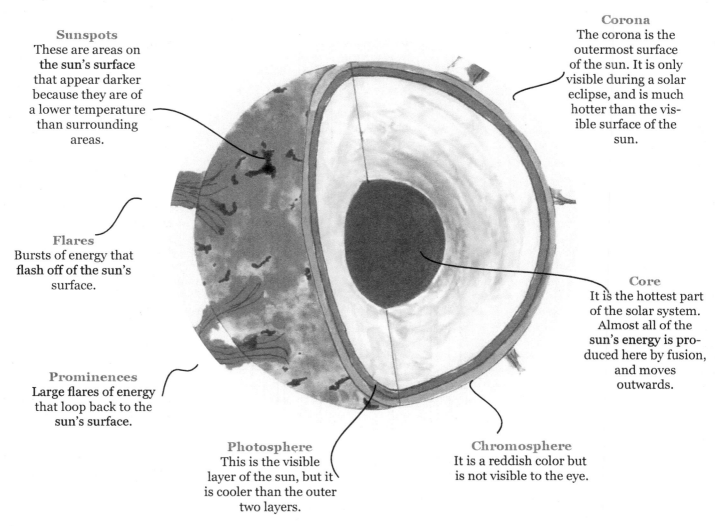

Sunspots
These are areas on the sun's surface that appear darker because they are of a lower temperature than surrounding areas.

Corona
The corona is the outermost surface of the sun. It is only visible during a solar eclipse, and is much hotter than the visible surface of the sun.

Flares
Bursts of energy that flash off of the sun's surface.

Core
It is the hottest part of the solar system. Almost all of the sun's energy is produced here by fusion, and moves outwards.

Prominences
Large flares of energy that loop back to the sun's surface.

Photosphere
This is the visible layer of the sun, but it is cooler than the outer two layers.

Chromosphere
It is a reddish color but is not visible to the eye.

Questions

What is the difference between a flare and a prominence?

What part of the sun produces the majority of heat and light?

What two parts of the sun's outer layer are only visible from Earth during a solar eclipse?

Why are sunspots darker than surrounding areas?

What part of the sun do we see from Earth?

How Does a Tree Live and Grow?

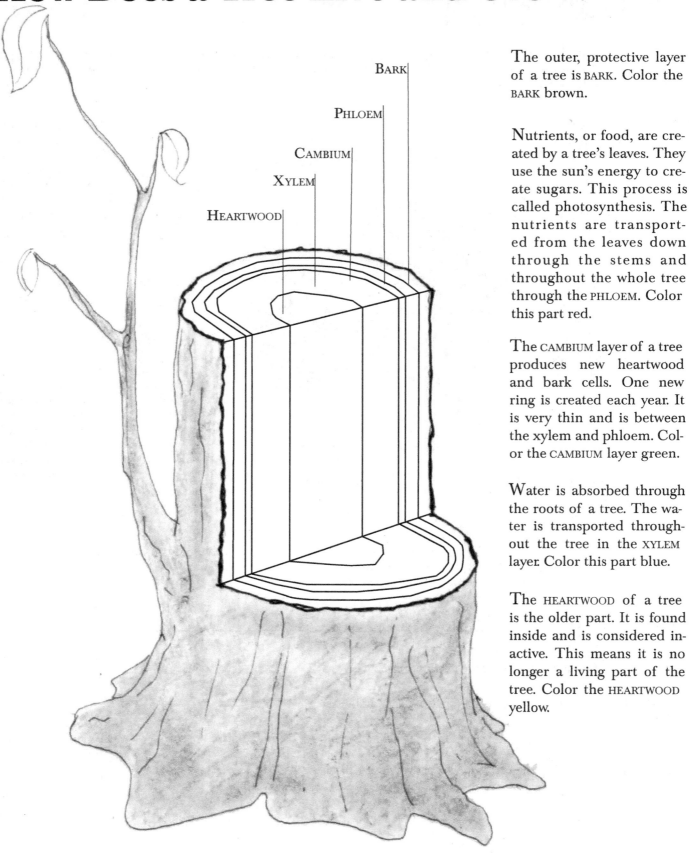

The outer, protective layer of a tree is BARK. Color the BARK brown.

Nutrients, or food, are created by a tree's leaves. They use the sun's energy to create sugars. This process is called photosynthesis. The nutrients are transported from the leaves down through the stems and throughout the whole tree through the PHLOEM. Color this part red.

The CAMBIUM layer of a tree produces new heartwood and bark cells. One new ring is created each year. It is very thin and is between the xylem and phloem. Color the CAMBIUM layer green.

Water is absorbed through the roots of a tree. The water is transported throughout the tree in the XYLEM layer. Color this part blue.

The HEARTWOOD of a tree is the older part. It is found inside and is considered inactive. This means it is no longer a living part of the tree. Color the HEARTWOOD yellow.

BARK

PHLOEM

CAMBIUM

XYLEM

HEARTWOOD

Learn *About* Tornadoes

A tornado is a spiraling _____ of air that reaches from a cloud to land. Tornadoes can reach speeds of up to _____ miles per hour and can cause significant destruction! In the _____ there are about 1,000 tornadoes each year. Most of these tornadoes occur in an area called Tornado Alley. Tornado Alley is right in the middle of the country and includes the states Texas, Kansas and _____

Most tornadoes form during _____ . When warm, moist air and cool, dry air mix the atmosphere becomes unstable. With a change in wind speed and direction a spinning effect begins to take place.

Rising air within this _____ tilts the rotating air into a vertical position. This column of rotating air is usually between two and six miles wide. _____ clouds can form within this area. When a funnel cloud reaches the _____

it is called a tornado.

Learn About Hurricanes

Use the word bank to fill the empty spaces in the paragraph.

WORD BANK

ISLANDS
HUMID
OCEAN
ENERGY
RAIN
MILES
WINDS
SPIRALS

    A hurricane is a huge storm that forms over the open _____. Hurricanes are made up of strong _____ and are usually accompanied by heavy _____. They can create large waves and cause a great amount of damage. Because a hurricane only travels over open ocean waters the places _____ and coastal towns. Hurricanes are formed most at risk are over ocean water that is 80° F or warmer. The warm water provides _____ for the hurricane. Winds come together above the water and force the air upward. _____ air, which is hot and moist, rises from the water to create storm-clouds. Above the storm clouds wind flows outward and allows the air to rise. The wind _____ around and around the storm. This storm becomes a hurricane when the cyclone reaches wind speeds of at least 74 _____ per hour.

58

Oxygen is number 8 on the periodic table of elements and its symbol is O. It is one of the most important elements of life. It is a **part of water and makes up more than 20% of our atmosphere.** It is also the most important part of air that we breathe in. Our lungs take it out of the air and transport it into our blood stream. Oxygen is also a very important part of inorganic materials. It is found in many metallic compounds and minerals that we use every day. Below, interpret each diagram and match it to the correct compound.

O_2

Molecular Oxygen - This is two oxygen atoms bonded together. It is the form of oxygen that makes up 20% of our atmosphere. It is also the form of oxygen that we breathe in and is absorbed into our bloodstream.

H_2O

Water - Water is everywhere and is essential to life. It covers more than 70% of the Earth's surface. It is a very simple molecule with two hydrogen atoms and one oxygen atom. A fish's gills can get oxygen out of water the way animals' lungs get it out of the air.

Fe_2O_3

Iron Oxide - This is a part of what makes rust. When iron combines with oxygen in the atmosphere the structure of the molecule changes and becomes a new substance.

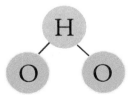

O_3

Ozone- This is another form of oxygen found in the atmosphere. But our bodies cannot use it when we breathe it in. It is very important in other ways though. Large quantities of ozone exist in our upper atmosphere and block the sun's radiation.

Pollination

Pollination is very important and neccessary to the reproduction of plants. There are several stems within a flower. These are called **stamen**. At the top of each stamen is a small pad where **pollen** sits. At the center of a flower there is a tube. The top of the tube is a sticky platform called a **stigma**. Pollen from the stamen must be transported to the stigma. This is typically done when bees and other insects feed on the nectar of the flower. The pollen sticks to the feeding bee. When the bee flies away to feed on another flower, it carries the pollen from the first flower to the stigma of the second flower. From the stigma pollen travels through a tube called the **pistil** down to the base of the flower. At the base of the flower is the **ovule**. That is where the pollen mixes with the other reproductive elements of the flower to make the seeds for new plants. It is important that the pollen of one flower reaches the stigma of the other. This creates diversity in the new plant's genes. Diversity means the new plant will not not inherit all the traits of either of its parents so it is less likely to inherit any problems they might have had.

First, find the different parts of the flower in the diagram; label and color them in. Color the stamen black, the pollen yellow, the stigma red, the pistil green and the ovule blue. Then with a blue line trace the path the bee must take to pollinate these two flowers. Using a green line trace the path the pollen takes to create new seeds with a different plant.

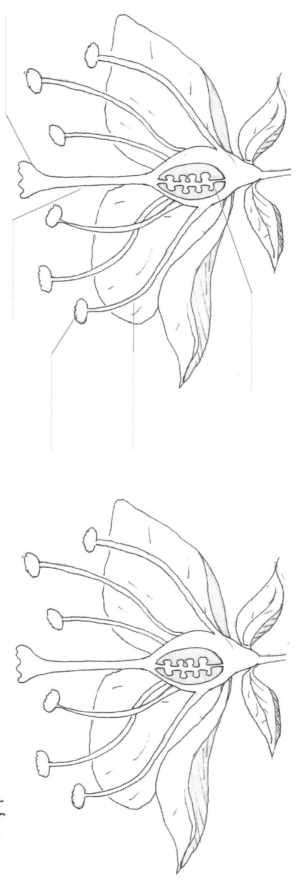

Carbon is number 6 on the periodic table of elements and its symbol is C. It is the most important element in organic material and without it life-forms cannot exist. Carbon appears in many compounds that are essential to living creatures, including carbon dioxide (CO_2) and methane (CH_4). By itself it can be a diamond, which is one of the hardest substances on Earth, and it can also be graphite, which is very soft and is used for writing. Below, interpret each diagram and match it to the correct compound.

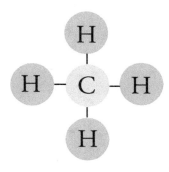

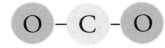

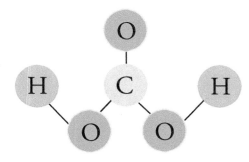

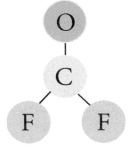

COF_2

Carbonyl Fluoride - This is a gas made of the elements carbon, oxygen and fluorine. It is highly toxic to human beings. It is used to produce other chemicals that contain fluorine.

CH_4

Methane - This is the simplest possible organic compound. It is made of carbon and hydrogen, the two most important elements in organic material.

H_2CO_3

Carbonic Acid - This is an inorganic acid. It is most often created when carbon dioxide (CO_2) is dissolved in water (H_2O). Our bodies use it to help transport CO_2 out of our bodies.

CO

Carbon Monoxide - This is a compound made of one oxygen atom and one carbon atom. It is a gas and is slightly lighter than air. It is toxic in high quantities but animal bodies produce small amounts of it.

CO_2

Carbon Dioxide - This is a gas made of one carbon atom and two oxygen atoms. Plants use this to create sugars through photosynthesis and animals release it when they breathe out.

Explore Hurricanes!

Anyone who has ever lived through a **hurricane** knows that they are the biggest, baddest storm nature can dish out. A large **hurricane** can grow to be *600 miles* across and packs the power of *many* nuclear bombs. These super-storms unleash high winds and rain on states like Florida and Louisiana year after year.

In contrast to the tremendous power they have when they arrive on American shores, **hurricanes** start in a simple way. A normal thunderstorm in North Africa will blow out into the Atlantic Ocean, near the earth's equator. Once the storm is over the water, it will begin to gain *more* power. The water around the equator collects a lot of solar energy, which adds to the storm's power. Hot air rises up the center of the thunderstorm, cooling off as it makes contact with a colder atmosphere and dumping moisture. **All that energy only adds to the storm**.

This exchange of hot air and moisture creates a giant column of air. As the storm picks up more energy, a rotation will form, causing the storm to start spinning faster and faster, picking up wind speeds. **As soon as the winds begin to blow at 75 mph or more, a hurricane is born**.

How does a hurricane move from the Atlantic Ocean to North America? Over the summer, trade winds blow from Africa to the United States. These winds *push* newly formed **hurricanes** across the Atlantic, helping the storm build up power. By the time the storm reaches the United States, its winds will have reached speeds of 100 mph or *more*.

Once a storm hits the U.S. the storm can *"come undone"* or the winds can shift and blow the **hurricane** harmlessly up the coast. In worst-case scenarios, the storm will hit land and cause massive damage to land and property. The storm's strong winds are capable of ripping out trees from the ground, and producing 1-2 feet of rainwater in less than a day. Over the course of one season, a **hurricane** will often leave some towns flooded and devastated.

Historical Hurricanes

1900
Galveston Hurricane
This hurricane hit Texas with winds of 145 mph. It is estimated about 6,000 - 12,000 people were killed.

1969
Hurricane Camille
The 2nd of three category 5 hurricanes to make landfall in the U.S. during the 20th century. This storm is also the first named after a person.

1992
Hurricane Andrew
This storm caused $26.5 billion in damages across Florida and Louisiana.

2005
Hurricane Katrina
One of the deadliest hurricanes in U.S. history, Katrina killed over 1,000 people and cost $81 billion in damages.

Safety Tips

1. Help your family put together a disaster kit.
2. Keep records of your valuables.
3. Plan an evacuation route with your family.
4. Keep an emergency radio.
5. During a storm, stay clear of electrical wires.
6. Research ways to secure and prepare your home.
7. If major flooding occurs, try staying above the water.

Explore Hurricanes!

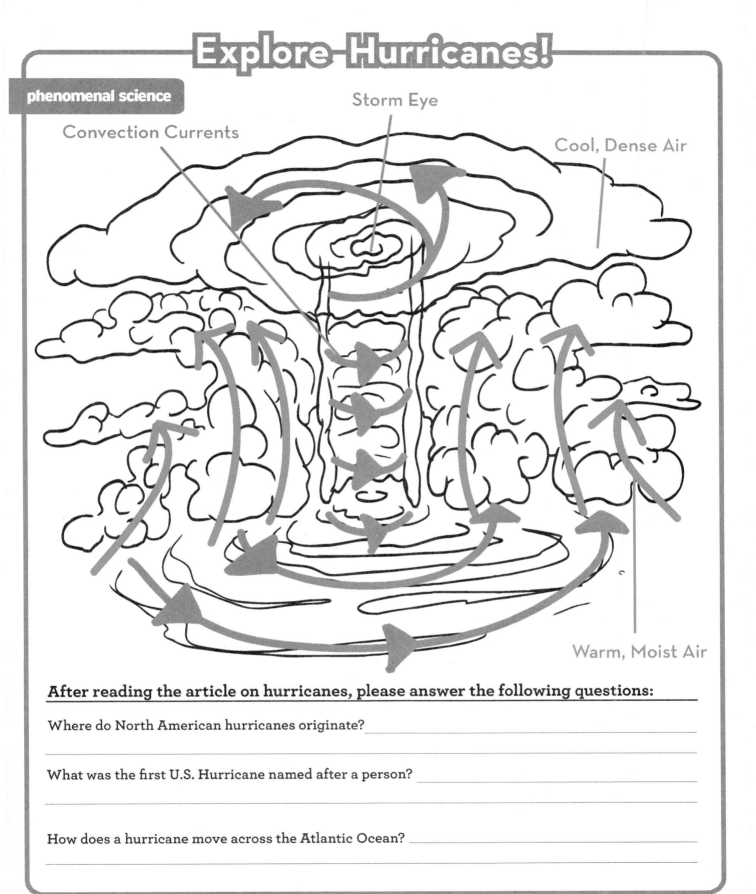

Storm Eye

Convection Currents

Cool, Dense Air

Warm, Moist Air

After reading the article on hurricanes, please answer the following questions:

Where do North American hurricanes originate?

What was the first U.S. Hurricane named after a person?

How does a hurricane move across the Atlantic Ocean?

Explore Tsunamis!

On **December 26th, 2004**, a massive **tsunami** rose from the Indian Ocean. This **tsunami** was one of the most destructive natural disasters anyone had ever seen before. Where did these disastrous waves come from, and how was this **tsunami** able to hit so quickly, without warning?

There are several different situations that can cause a **tsunami**: **underwater volcanic eruptions**, **meteor strikes**, **coastal landslides**, and, most commonly, **underwater earthquakes**.

Earthquakes that cause **tsunamis** involve the earth's **tectonic plates**. These plates are constantly moving over and under one another. The upper plate can get stuck on the lower one, building pressure. When the pressure grows large enough, the upper plate will snap upwards *very* quickly. When the plate snaps up by several inches, it also pushes an entire section of the ocean with it. This part of the ocean will suddenly be several inches above sea level. Once this spike happens, the water will spread out in order to restore equilibrium. This bump will spread out with incredible speed, moving at *hundreds of miles per hour*. When the wave reaches the shallower waters of the coast, the compressed energy of the wave will transform it into a **tsunami**. A typical **tsunami** approaching land will slow down to speeds of 30mph as the wave grows to *heights of up to 90ft above sea level*. A **tsunami** almost always promises flooding, destruction, and sometimes loss of life.

Scientists have the equipment to detect underwater earthquakes, just before a **tsunami** can hit the coast. However, because these giant waves form so quickly and hit coastal areas at hundreds of miles per hour, these detections often come too late. If you live near the coast, be aware of **tsunami zones**. Make sure your family has a plan in case you are caught near the wave.

Historical Tsunamis

1755 — **Lisbon Tsunami**
Following the devastating Lisbon earthquake, the tsunami nearly destroyed the Portuguese city of Lisbon.

1883 — **Krakatoa Tsunami**
The volcanic island of Krakatoa destroyed two-thirds of the Indonesian island, and sent high waves across the Indian Ocean, killing 36,000 people.

2004 — **Indonesian Tsunami**
Over 230,000 people in 14 countries died after this tsunami hit. It was one of the deadliest natural disasters in recorded history.

2011 — **Tohoku Tsunami**
Following one of the most powerful earthquakes, a series of giant tsunamis hit Japan. The disaster cost Japan 15,000 lives and $235 billion in economic loss.

Safety Tips

1. If you live near the coast, look up your local tsunami broadcast.

2. Be aware of nature's warning signs. Tsunamis often follow after earthquakes, landslides near the coast, volcanic eruptions, and meteor strikes.

3. If you see a tsunami happening, leave the beach immediately and go to higher ground.

4. If you don't have an emergency kit, help your family put together one that includes a first aid kit, a supply of fresh water and canned food.

Explore Tsunamis!

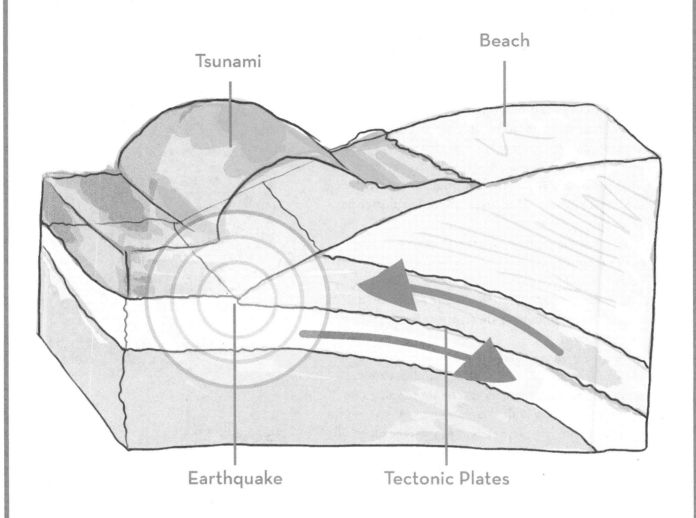

Tsunami

Beach

Earthquake

Tectonic Plates

After reading the article on tsunamis, please answer the following questions:

Name two different events that would cause a tsunami.

How do tectonic plates cause earthquakes?

What are some ways you can prepare for a tsunami?

Explore Earthquakes!

Have you ever felt an earthquake? If you have, you'd know it's a sickening feeling. It seems impossible that the entire earth can move so dramatically, but during an **earthquake** it actually does.

So how does the ground shake and move the way it does during an **earthquake?** In order to answer that question, it's important to know exactly what is happening. An **earthquake** is a vibration that travels through the earth's crust. **A volcanic eruption, a large meteor impact,** or any sort of **big underground explosion** can create that vibration.

The most common cause of **earthquakes** are the earth's **tectonic plates.** These plates are in constant motion and when they bump into one another it can cause underground vibrations. Each year, more than *three million earthquakes* are an after effect of **tectonic plates** moving.

There are different ways for plates to interact with each other. In a **normal fault,** the plates are separating. In a **reverse fault,** the plates are running into each other. In a **slip fault,** the plates move in opposite directions, with one plate sliding against the other. **Slip faults** cause the most dramatic **earthquakes.** The edges of these plates can actually lock together as they slide against each other, building up pressure. Then, in an instant, the pressure releases.

When the shift occurs in the earth's crust, the energy radiates **seismic waves.** These waves are like waves of water in a pond, but here the waves radiate through the earth and make the ground shake. There are three kinds of waves: **P waves, S waves,** and **L waves. P waves** cause the thud in the beginning of the quake, while **S waves** and **L waves** cause the most damage because they both move plate foundations.

The largest **earthquake** ever registered on earth measured 9.5 on the **Richter scale. Earthquakes** that register at 3 aren't usually felt by humans. For us to feel an **earthquake,** it must measure around 5 on the **Richter scale.**

Historical Earthquakes

1811 — **Madrid Missouri Quakes**
These earthquakes happened along the Mississippi River, lasting for months. These quakes actually caused the river to run backwards.

1906 — **San Francisco Earthquake**
One of the most famous U.S. disasters, the fires started by this earthquake actually did more damage than the quake itself.

1970 — **Ancash Earthquake**
One of the biggest earthquakes ever recorded, the Ancash earthquake caused landslides, destroyed homes and took away many lives. This quake hit 7.8 on the Richter scale.

Safety Tips

1. Stay away from windows.
2. Stay indoors.
3. Take cover under a sturdy piece of furniture.
4. Secure shelves and heavy objects against the wall.
5. Plan an earthquake preparation kit with your family.
6. If advised to evacuate, do so immediately.
7. Stay away from electrical wires.

Explore Earthquakes!

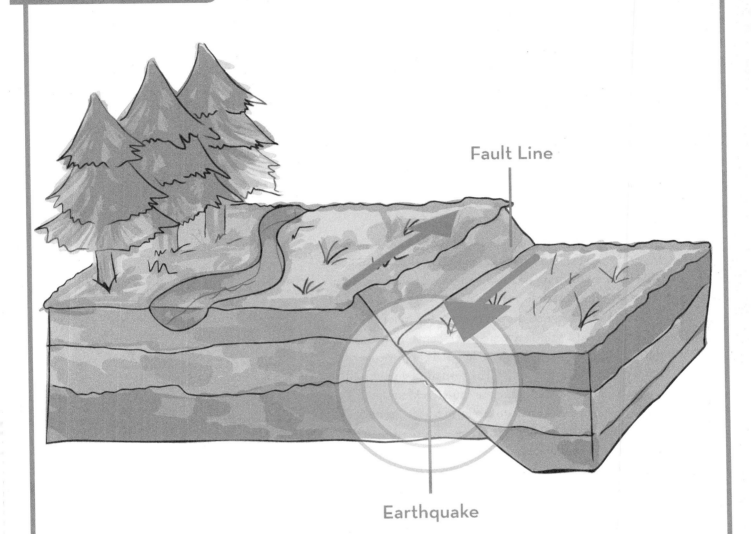

Fault Line

Earthquake

After reading the article on earthquakes, please answer the following questions:

Name two different events that would cause an earthquake.

What are the three ways tectonic plates interact with each other?

What are seismic waves?

Explore Tornadoes!

A **tornado** is an amazing, awesome act of nature that can leave citizens dumbfounded. It's a huge, swirling, beast of a storm that can appear to have a mind of its own.

Tornadoes start with a massive thundercloud. The cloud sucks huge amounts of air up its center. In the largest clouds, called **super cells**, there is enough energy in that upswelling of air to spawn a **tornado**. As warm, wet air collides with cool, dry air, the storm will spin faster and faster. It finally twists down to the ground, creating a **tornado**.

If you've ever seen a whirlpool form in a drain, you have seen how a **tornado** works. A drain's whirlpool, also known as a **vortex**, forms because of the down draft that the drain creates in the body of water. The downward flow of water into the drain begins to rotate, and as the rotation speeds up, the **vortex** forms.

Tornadoes move and devour the ground, following a path controlled by the thundercloud it came from. Sometimes the **tornado** will appear to hop. The hops occur when the **vortex** is disturbed. The **tornado's vortex** will hop, form, and collapse along the thundercloud's path.

Scientists measure **tornado** strength on the **Fujita Scale**, also known as the **F-Scale**. Wind speeds are estimated by the damage accumulated from a **tornado**. Once those wind speeds are established, a **tornado** can be placed on the **F-Scale**. The weakest **tornadoes** are rated **F-0** with wind speeds of up to 72MPH. **F-2 tornadoes** can tear roofs from houses and destroy mobile homes. **F-4 tornadoes** are able to toss cars up in the sky with winds of up to 260mph. **F-5 tornadoes** bring total devastation at over 300 mph; no faster winds have ever been recorded by scientists. An **F-5 tornado** can pick up a cow and launch it as a projectile.

Despite modern radar technology, experts cannot predict exactly when and where a **tornado** will touch down. It's important to pay attention to emergency broadcasts if you live in a **tornado zone**. Should a **tornado** happen where you live, the safest place to be is an underground storm shelter with a very strong door such as a basement or emergency shelter.

Historical Tornadoes

1840 — **Great Natchez Tornado**
The 2nd deadliest tornado in U.S. history, this storm killed 317 people and injured 109.

1925 — **Tri-State Tornado**
This giant storm left the longest recorded track in the world at 219 miles in length.

1974 — **Super Outbreak**
Over 148 tornadoes hit 13 states, with nearly 30 of the tornadoes ranked on the Fujita Scale as F5.

2011 — **Joplin Tornado**
One of the costliest single tornadoes in U.S. history, the cost to rebuild after the Joplin disaster reached $3 billion.

Safety Tips

1. Seek shelter immediately during a tornado.
2. Keep away from windows.
3. Keep away from electric sockets and wires.
4. Keep an emergency radio.
5. Move to a basement or under a sturdy table.
6. Research ways to secure and prepare your home.
7. Lie face down on the ground and cover yourself.

Explore Tornadoes!

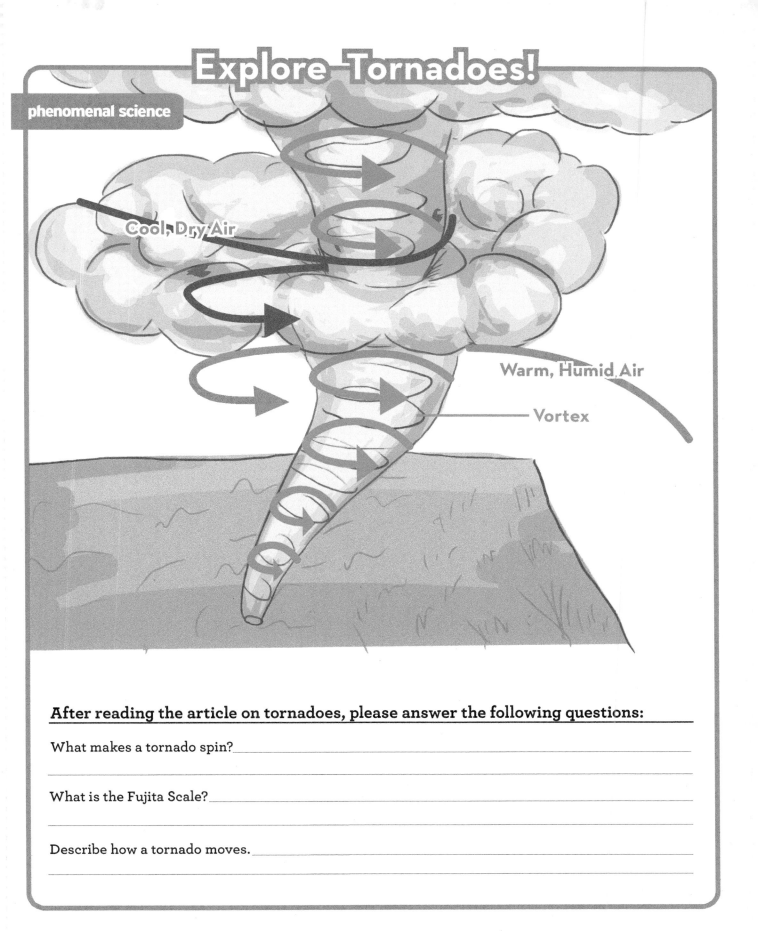

Cool, Dry Air

Warm, Humid Air

Vortex

After reading the article on tornadoes, please answer the following questions:

What makes a tornado spin?_____

_____

What is the Fujita Scale?_____

_____

Describe how a tornado moves._____

_____

Great job!

is an Education.com reading superstar

EVERYDAY PHYSICS

What is Sound?

Sound is made with vibrations. Whenever an object vibrates it causes air particles to move and bump into each other in wave-like motions. We call these vibrations *sound waves*. Just like water ripples when you throw a stone into it, sound waves ripple and keep going until they run out of energy. Our ears vibrate in a similar way to the original source of the sound. This is how we hear many different sounds.

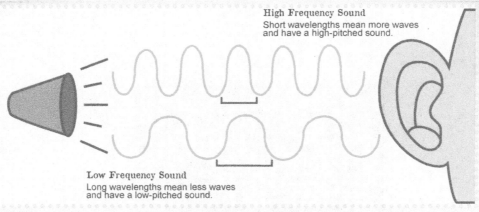

High Frequency Sound
Short wavelengths mean more waves and have a high-pitched sound.

Low Frequency Sound
Long wavelengths mean less waves and have a low-pitched sound.

Describe the frequencies you see below. What kind of sound do you think they are making?

_____   _____

_____   _____

_____   _____

TRY THIS!

Have you ever tried to make a pretty tone by rubbing the rim of a wine glass? When you wet your finger and drag it around the rim, it slips and sticks to the glass—similar to the way a violin bow slips and sticks to the strings that it plays. This "slip-stick" motion causes the glass to start vibrating. Try adding more water to the glass. What happens to the tone?

THINK ABOUT IT!

Do you think there is sound in space? Why or why not?
Hint: Space is a vacuum, which means that there are no air particles.

Moving Sound The Doppler Effect

Ever notice how sound changes and warps as it gets nearer or farther away? For instance, as a train comes closer the sound is high pitched, and it increases in pitch until it passes you. Then when it passes the pitch drops very quickly. This is called the Doppler effect.

WHAT'S HAPPENING?

The Doppler effect happens because the air in front of a moving object is compressed. That means the air particles are closer together, so the sound waves are closer together and create a high-pitched frequency. The air behind a moving object is not compressed.

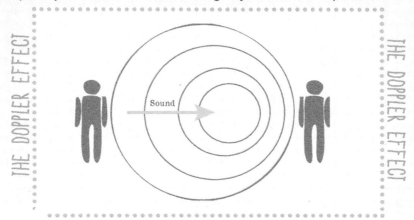

THINK ABOUT IT!

We are most familiar with the Doppler effect because of our experiences with sound waves. Perhaps you recall an instance in which a police car or emergency vehicle was traveling towards you on the highway. What do you remember happening as the car passed by? Why do you think that is? Draw an example using the diagram above to show a police car driving by with the sound waves!

_____

_____

_____

_____

_____

DID YOU KNOW?

The Doppler effect is actually very useful for astronomers. They are able to get lots of information about stars and galaxies by studying the frequencies of electromagnetic waves that are produced by moving stars.

Speed of Sound

Sound travels at different speeds, depending on how fast the vibrations are passed from particle to particle. Because of this, sound travels at different speeds through different materials.

A)

MATERIAL	SPEED OF SOUND
Rubber	60 meters/second
Air	340 meters/second
Lead	1210 meters/second
Glass	4540 meters/second
Aluminum	6320 meters/second

B)

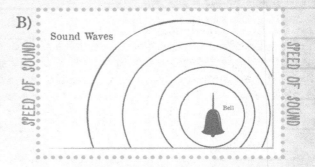

THINK ABOUT IT! (Use chart A for the following questions)

Why does sound travel at different speeds through different materials?

_____

_____

In chart A, what material does sound move through the fastest? Why do you think this happens?

_____

_____

_____

CHALLENGE QUESTION

If a sound wave travels through the air at approximately 750 miles per hour, how many seconds does it take for that sound wave to travel one mile?
Hint: Speed = Distance ÷ Time

DID YOU KNOW?

Researchers who looked at results from the 2004 Olympics say sprinters who were closest to the gun took off faster, probably because they perceived the shot faster and louder than their competitors did.

Speed of Light

In outer space, where there are no air particles, the speed of light is 299,792,458 meters per second. That is approximately 186,000 miles per second!

DID YOU KNOW?

The starlight we see in the night sky is actually tens to hundreds of years old! Although their light travels very fast across the vacuum of space, the stars are so far away that their light takes many years to reach Earth. Light travels much faster than sound.

In fact, the sun's light takes 8 minutes to reach us on Earth. In theory, if the sun were to go out, we wouldn't know until 8 minutes after it happened.

The length of time it takes light to go from:

Moon to Earth:
1.2 seconds

Earth to Sun:
8.5 seconds

THINK ABOUT IT:

Why do we count the seconds in between the lightning flash and the sound of the thunder?

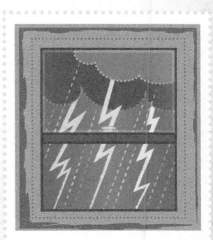

_____

_____

_____

_____

_____

Air Resistance

All matter has substance/mass, even air molecules!
Air resistance (or *drag*) happens when air molecules
collide with a moving object and slow it down.

EXAMPLE: A skydiver who jumps out of a plane.

DID YOU KNOW?

When a car travels at 50 miles per hour or more,
half of the gas it uses is spent on overcoming
air resistance!

Dimples on a golf ball help reduce drag, allowing the
ball to fly further than a ball without dimples.

Air Resistance

Weight

WATER RESISTANCE:

Today's competitive swimwear has changed so drastically that the material goes
faster through the water than human skin. Controversy over the new suits has broken
out, due to the fact that consistent world record times have been broken since
the introduction of new water-resistant material starting around the year 2000.

THINK ABOUT IT!

If you were to drop 2 dollar bills, one crumpled and one flat, the crumpled one would fall faster
because there is less resistance acting on the paper. Air resistance works with an object's surface
area. The more of an area the more air resistance!

Air Resistance (continued)

READING COMPREHENSION

1. What factors affect air resistance?

_____

_____

_____

_____

2. What directions do the forces of <u>air resistance</u> and <u>weight</u> act on a falling object?

_____

_____

_____

3. If a skydiver jumps out of a plane, which force is greater - gravity or air resistance?

_____

_____

_____

4. Why does a feather fall slower than a tennis ball?

_____

_____

Paper Airplane Physics

AERODYNAMICS — Have you ever held your hand out of the car window on the freeway? If you hold your palm out with your fingertips toward the sky, the wind fights your hand. This is called *air resistance*. If you hold your hand flat with your fingertips facing the direction that the car is moving, the wind travels smoothly over your hand. That is *aerodynamic*s.

DRAG — For a far and fast flight, less drag is better! Drag is the pull you feel when the air resists your open palm.

GRAVITY — The plane is constantly being pulled down by gravity. The lighter the plane, the better the flight.

THRUST — This is the forward movement of the plane, as you launch it.

LIFT — This is the upward movement of the plane, which comes from the airplane's wings. If the air below the wing is pushing up harder than the air above the wing, the plane will have more lift!

THE FOUR FORCES IN BALANCE

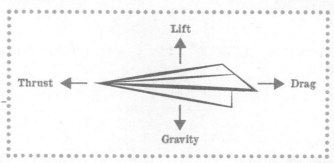

NOW IT'S YOUR TURN
Basic Paper Glider

1. Fold the two upper corners down.

3. Take the two outer corners and fold like this:

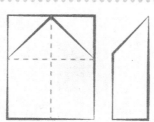

2. Fold paper in half length-wise.

4. Your glider should look like this!

Friction

WHAT IS FRICTION?

It is a force that happens when two objects are touching and move across or against each other.

THINK ABOUT IT!

Why does an "Indian burn" hurt so badly?

_____
_____
_____
_____
_____

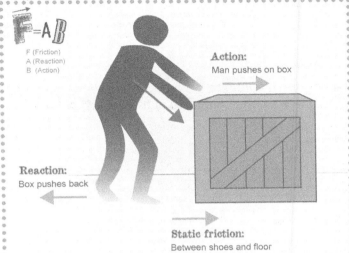

F = A B

F (Friction)
A (Reaction)
B (Action)

Action:
Man pushes on box

Reaction:
Box pushes back

Static friction:
Between shoes and floor

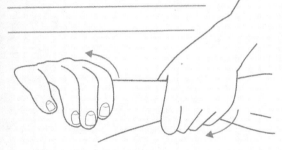

FRICTION CAUSES *heat*...!

Have you ever tried to rub two sticks together to make a fire? It takes a long time!

CHALLENGE QUESTION!

What modern technology do we have to make fire? Does it involve friction?

_____
_____
_____
_____
_____

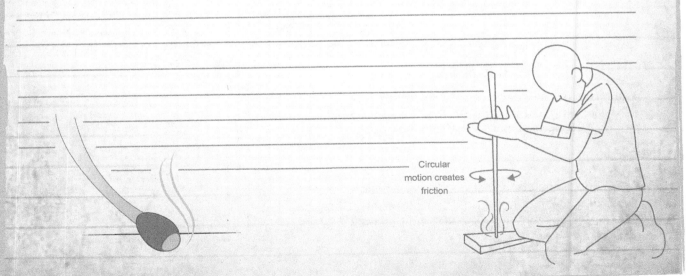

Circular motion creates friction

Gravity Newton's Law of Gravitation

All objects that have mass are attracted to each other.

NEWTON'S LAW OF UNIVERSAL GRAVITATION: Every object in the universe attracts every other object with a force directed along the line of centers for the two objects.

> Gravity pulls **ALL** objects towards the earth at the same rate of speed!

THINK ABOUT IT!

Using the diagram to the right, explain what you see. Will the watermelon hit first or the apple? Why?

_____
_____
_____
_____
_____
_____

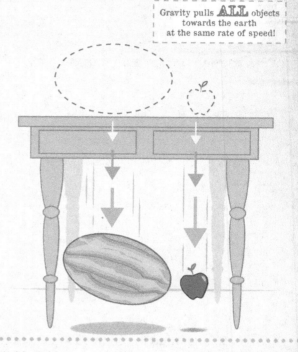

WHAT CAUSES THINGS TO ORBIT?

An orbit happens when there is a perfect balance between the forward motion of a body in space, such as a planet or moon, and the pull of gravity from another body in space, such as a large planet or star. An object with a lot of mass moves forward; however, the gravity of another body in space pulls. It's a continuous tug-of-war between the two objects.

DID YOU KNOW?

The moon doesn't circle around the earth. It is actually falling towards the Earth. It does not crash into us because it is held in an orbit by gravity.

FUN FACT:

Weight depends on how strong the gravitational pull is. You'll weigh less or more on different planets. Because of differences in gravity, a 220-pound person would only weigh 84 pounds on Mars.

Newton's First Law The Law of Inertia

THE LAW OF INERTIA

An object at rest will remain at rest unless acted on by an unbalanced force. An object in motion continues in motion with the same speed and in the same direction unless acted upon by an unbalanced force.

THINK ABOUT IT!

This is why you wear a seatbelt in the car!

The sled only starts moving when someone gives it a push down the hill.

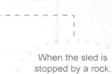

When the sled is stopped by a rock, the kid keeps going and flies off of it!

CHALLENGE QUESTIONS!

1. Which objects are in motion in this picture?

_____

_____

2. What is the unbalanced force in this picture?

_____

_____

3. What happened to the sledder in this picture?

_____

_____

4. Describe an experience you have had relating to Newton's Law of Inertia.

_____

_____

Newton's Second Law The Law of Acceleration

ACCELERATION is produced when a force acts on a mass. The greater the mass of the object being accelerated, the greater amount of force needed to accelerate the object.

N?   1,500 kg   .07 m/s/s

Phillip's car weighs 1,500 kg. He just ran out of gas and needs to push the car to a gas station and he makes the car go 0.07 m/s/s. Using Newton's Second Law, how much force is Phillip applying to the car?

F=MA

F= 1,500 x 0.07

Answer: _____

THINK ABOUT IT!

The heavier the object the more force you will need in order to move it compared to a lighter object, which requires less force.

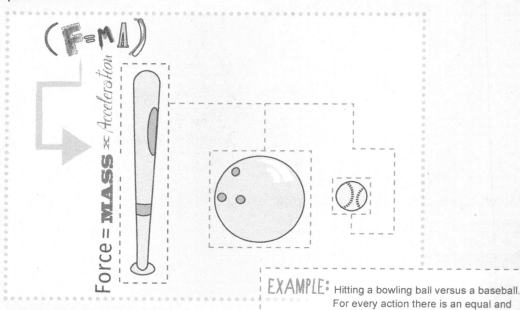

(F=MA)

Force = **MASS** ∝ Acceleration

EXAMPLE: Hitting a bowling ball versus a baseball. For every action there is an equal and opposite reaction. When you push an object, it pushes back.

CHALLENGE QUESTION!

What would happen if you hit a baseball with a bat? A bowling ball? Describe the difference.

_____

_____

_____

_____

Newton's Third Law of Motion The Action-Reaction Law

ACTION-REACTION LAW
To every action there is always an equal and opposite reaction.

THINK ABOUT IT!

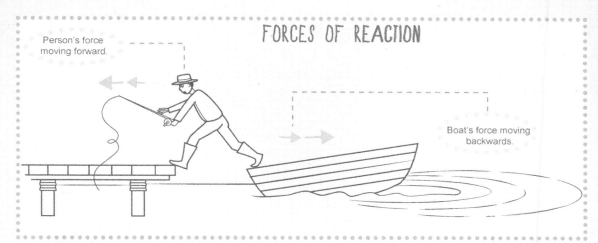

Person's force moving forward.

FORCES OF REACTION

Boat's force moving backwards.

CHALLENGE QUESTIONS!

1. You're driving down the road, and a bug hits the windshield of the car! The bug hits the car and the car hits the bug. Which of the two forces is greater: The force on the bug or the force on the car?

_____

_____

_____

2. Many people know that a rifle recoils, or jerks back when fired. This is the result of Newton's action-reaction law. A gunpowder blast creates hot gases that expand outward allowing the rifle to push forward on the bullet, and the bullet pushes backwards upon the rifle. The acceleration of the recoiling rifle is _____ than the acceleration of the bullet.:

   a) greater
   b) smaller
   c) the same size

What is Energy?

Energy is the ability of one object to do work on another object. Usually energy is defined as a force that acts over a distance.

Most types of energy fall under two categories: *kinetic energy or potential energy.* Kinetic energy is the energy that an object has when it's in motion. Potential energy is the stored energy in an object that is at rest. Forces like gravity and electric charge are what give all objects in this world potential energy.

The law of conservation of energy states that energy cannot be destroyed or created; it can only be transferred or transformed.

Some types of energy are: wind energy, chemical energy, solar energy, nuclear energy, geothermal energy, sound energy, hydro energy, elastic potential energy, gravitational potential energy.

DID YOU KNOW?

Over 1,000 homes can be powered for one year with 1 million tons of garbage. If all garbage in the United States was converted to energy it could power a city for one year.

If 10,000 schools turned off their lights for one minute it could save $81,885.

The amount of energy Americans use *doubles* about every 20 years.

Volcanoes and geysers are examples of geothermal energy.

What is Energy? (continued)

MATCH THE ENERGY!

Match the type of energy that goes with the correct picture! Types: wind energy, chemical energy, solar energy, nuclear energy, geothermal energy, sound energy, hydro energy, elastic potential energy, gravitational potential energy.

Energy

E = mc²

WHAT'S HAPPENING?

We all know this famous equation. But what does it all mean?

Two of the most important parts of physical science are matter and energy. Matter is anything that takes up space. Energy is the property of matter that performs work. Matter and energy are two forms of the same thing. Einstein created a mathematical formula that explains how matter can be changed into energy.

E = eneRgy

m = mass

c^2 = speed of light times the speed of light.

electromagnetic force
nuclear forces

$E = mc^2$

E (energy) equals m (mass) times c2
(c stands for the speed of light).

This equation allows scientists to know how much energy things have, whether it's the energy in a bowling ball or the energy in a supernova.

THINK ABOUT IT!

How do you think the following items use energy?

A growing tree: _____

A person: _____

A toaster: _____

A light bulb: _____

DID YOU KNOW?

Stars shine because the matter inside them is slowly being changed back into energy.

The Physics of Lightning

What is happening when lightning strikes the ground?

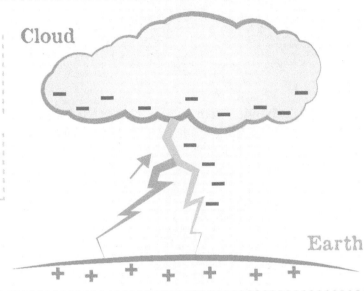

Cloud

Earth

As the negative charges approach the ground, a stream of positive charges repelled by the ground attract to the negative stream.

When connected, they have created a path which allows a sudden down surge of electrons to jump to the ground.

This is the lightning.

As the **NEGATIVE** charges collect at the bottom of the cloud it forces the negative charges in the ground to be forced away from the surface. This leaves the ground **POSITIVE.**

DID YOU KNOW?

Cars are a very safe place to be, and it's not the rubber tires that protect you! This is a very common misconception. It is actually the metal that is surrounding you that acts like a cage of protection. This is due to the Skin Effect which says that electricity, like lightning, will travel only on the surface of enclosed metal objects. So while your car may be hit by lightning, if you stay inside you will be safe.

CHALLENGE QUESTION: Why are you safer if you are lower to the ground?

_____

_____

_____

_____

FUN FACTS!

The temperature of a lightning flash is 15,000 to 60,000 degrees Fahrenheit. That's hotter than the surface of the sun (9,000 degrees Fahrenheit).

Condensation and Evaporation

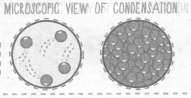

MICROSCOPIC VIEW OF CONDENSATION

Gas to a solid or liquid.

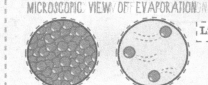

MICROSCOPIC VIEW OF EVAPORATION

Liquid to a gas.

WHAT'S THE DIFFERENCE?

Condensation is a warming effect. It changes from a vapor to a condensed state, either a solid or a liquid. Evaporation is a cooling effect—it's the change of a liquid to a gas.

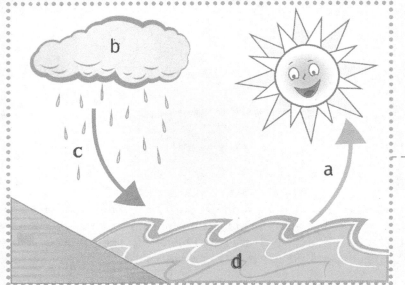

a: Evaporation
b: Condensation
c: Precipitation
d: Collection

THINK ABOUT IT!

When you're finished in the shower, it's wise to towel off with the curtains/doors still closed – the closed space traps the water vapor in. As the vapor condenses, it keeps you warm. But once you open up the curtains, all the gas will escape and you'll be left with water evaporating off of your body, making you colder.

FUN FACT:

When you sweat, your body knows it's too hot and sweats in order to cool itself. The moisture produced by your body evaporates and helps to cool off your skin.

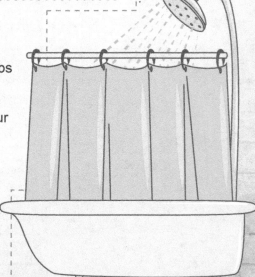

Condensation and Evaporation

CHALLENGE QUESTION:

1. Hanging Wet Clothes

Where do you think would be the best place to put your clothes/materials so that they will dry as quickly as possible? Draw a picture showing what you think will happen to the water.

_____

_____

_____

_____

_____

_____

_____

2. Condensation of Breath in Air

Describe what you think is happening when you can see your breath in the air. Where do you think it comes from? Do you think you can make it go away?

_____

_____

_____

_____

_____

_____

_____

_____

_____

Magnet Myths

Magnets are objects that create an area of magnetic force called a magnetic field. These fields by themselves are invisible to the human eye. Magnets only attract certain types of metals, such as iron, cobalt, and nickel.

Attracted to:
Iron
Cobalt
Nickel

NOT attracted to:
Plastic   Copper
Gold   Silver
Aluminum   Magnesium
Glass

Magnets have a north pole and a south pole. If the same poles of two magnets are put close to each other they will repel or push away. If different poles are close to each other they will be attracted to each other and pull together.

Magnetic objects must be inside the magnetic field to respond, which is why you may have to move a magnet closer for it to have an effect.

Unlike poles attract

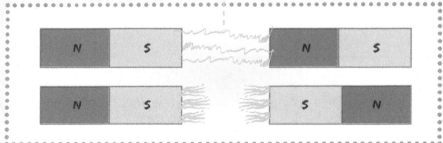

Like poles repel

FREQUENT QUESTIONS

Can a magnet damage electronics?

Yes, powerful magnets are actually used to wipe information from computer hard drives. Most types of electronic equipment are made with tiny magnets, and those can be affected by another magnet close by. However, most household magnets, such as fridge magnets, are not strong enough to damage electronics.

Can a magnet wipe information from a CD?

No. The information on a CD is burned onto the CD with a laser. A magnet won't affect the information on a CD.

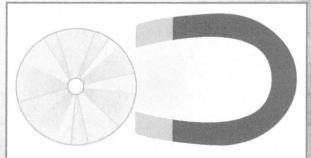

Magnet Myths (continued)

FREQUENT QUESTIONS...

Can you make a metal magnetic by Rubbing a magnet on it?

To make a metal magnetic, you must do something to manipulate the magnetic domains of the metal so that they point in the same direction. This happens when you rub a pin on a magnet – the pin's magnetic domains will align because they've been exposed to the magnet's magnetic field. You can also do this by placing a piece of metal in a strong magnetic field in a north-south direction or passing an electrical current through it.

Do magnets have healing powers?

Doctors and scientists have been studying the healing effects of magnets for a long time. But we're still not quite sure of how powerful a magnet's healing capabilities are. There are many theories to explain why magnets MIGHT be good for your body. For example, some say that the iron found in hemoglobin in your blood can be affected by magnets. That is why many people wear magnetic bracelets or necklaces to help improve blood circulation. Some say that magnets can also change the structure of nearby cells. This could mean that magnets might be able to heal pain or illnesses.

Magnets are used as a part of many different medical devices. For example, an MRI (Magnetic Resonance Imaging) uses magnetic fields to see the organs in our bodies.

COMPREHENSION

1. If you can manipulate metal to be magnetic, do you think you can demagnetize something? How would this work?

_____

_____

_____

2. Magnets do one of two things, repel or attract. Why is this?

_____

_____

_____

Super Hero Physics!

Now that you have learned all about physics, if you were a *Super Hero* what would your powers be?

_____

_____

_____

Would you rather be able to move at the speed of sound or the speed of light?

_____

_____

Who is Sound Man's arch nemesis?

_____

If you had the gift of super friction, what would you be able to do?

_____

_____

Lightning Boy is about to strike! Where will you hide?

_____

_____

Who does better in the water:
Sound Man or Light Man? What about in outer space?

_____

_____

_____

What special features does Air Resistance Man's super suit have?

_____

_____

Great job!

is an Education.com science superstar

Winter Olympics
BOBSLED

Try This!

Experiment with aerodynamics using a paper airplane made out of a sheet of 8.5 by 11 inch printer paper.

Think of the time when you're holding the airplane and winding up to send it sailing through the air as the push-off—for the plane to fly, the plane has to accelerate from rest just like the athletes must get the bobsled moving from rest at the starting line. Like the bobsledders during the push-off, you need to keep the motion of the plane straight and steady, or it'll crash right when you release it.

1. If the paper airplane is travelling fast and smoothly when you're holding it, it will continue to travel in the same way when you let it go. Practice throwing your airplane until you can get it to fly straight and steady several times in a row. Right now, your airplane is very aerodynamic.

2. Cut one-inch slits on each wing along the middle fold. Fold the two flaps upward so that they are at a 90 degree angle from the wing. Throw your modified plane several times.

How does the plane fly after you add the flaps? Does it fly as fast and far as before? Why?

The paper airplane floated more and did not go as fast when the flaps were added. This is because the flaps added drag to the airplane, making it less aerodynamic.

3. If an object has more mass, it also has more inertia. So when a massive body is in motion, forces of friction have less of an effect on its velocity. For this reason, bobsled teams want to maximize the amount of weight in the bobsled. The weight limit in the four-man bobsled is 630 kg (including athletes and sled). If the team doesn't reach that weight, they are allowed to add metal weights to the sled.

Add a paperclip to the nose of your airplane along the base fold. How does it fly? Why?

The airplane should fly faster, straighter, and steadier because the paperclip added mass — and inertia — to the airplane, making it more resistant to change in its motion and less affected by forces of friction like air resistance.

Winter Olympics
DOWNHILL SKIING

Downhill Skiing is less technical than slalom skiing. It involves fewer turns, but athletes ski at much higher speeds. Most courses exceed speeds of 81 mph, and the French athlete Johan Clarey broke the 100 mph barrier on a particularly fast course in 2013.

Check out the diagram illustrating the various forces acting on the downhill skier below. She has just triumphantly crossed the finish line, but she's still moving pretty fast! She now has to decelerate (slow down) until her momentum returns to zero. See how she's turned her skis perpendicular to the direction of her momentum? She does this so that she can exert force on the snow with her legs. The snow pushes back with an equal and opposite force, which slows her down. But to come to a complete stop, how much force would she have to exert on the snow, and for how long? Let's find out.

force of the athlete's legs pushing on the snow

force of the snow pushing back on the athlete

athlete's momentum

We'll pretend this particular athlete has a mass of 62 kilograms, and she crosses the finish line at a velocity of 28 meters per second. First, multiply mass and velocity together to get her momentum:

62 Kilograms x 28 m/s = 1736 newton-seconds

The unit we use to measure **momentum** is newton-seconds. Newton-seconds tell us that the athlete's momentum really just comes from force measured in newtons (in this case, gravity) acting on her over a certain amount of **time**, measured in **seconds**. Gravity has given this athlete a momentum of 1736 newton-seconds, so we know that she'll need to exert the same amount of force back on the snow in order to stop: 1736 newtons (which is the same as **390 pounds**) if she wanted to come to a complete stop in one second. Crazy, right? Fortunately, skiers usually have more time to stop than that!

Try This!

How much force is in a newton? Think of it this way: weight is just a measure of how much force gravity exerts on something. There are just over four newtons to a pound. To lift a 5 pound dumbbell, you need to exert just over 22 newtons on it. Practice converting newtons to pounds using the following equation:

1 pound = 4.45 newtons

If a bowling ball weighs 2.2 pounds, it also weighs 9.79 newtons.

If your bike weighs 30 pounds, it also weighs 133.5 newtons.

If your textbook weighs 3 pounds, it also weighs 13.35 newtons.

If you weigh _____ pounds, you also weigh _____ newtons. (answers will vary)

Winter Olympics
DOWNHILL SKIING

Try This!

Let's try to find out how much force each athlete would have to exert on the snow to come to a complete stop after crossing the finishing line.

Soo-ho, an athlete from the Republic of Korea, skis over the finish line at a speed of 32 meters per second. She weighs 62 kilograms. How much momentum does she have?

62 kilograms x 32 meters per second =
1984 newton-seconds

To find out the average force Soo-ho would have to exert on the snow to stop in three seconds, divide the above result by three:

Soo-ho would have to exert an average force of 661.33 newtons on the snow to come to a complete stop in 3 seconds.

Sigmund, an athlete from Norway, skis over the finish line at a speed of 40 meters per second. He weighs 81 kilograms. How much momentum does he have?

81kg x 40m/s = 3240 newton-seconds

To find out the average force Sigmund would have to exert on the snow to stop in three seconds, divide the above result by three:

Sigmund would have to exert an average force of 1080 newtons on the snow to come to a complete stop in 3 seconds.

Winter Olympics
SLALOM SKIING

Newton's first law says that any moving object wants to continue moving in a straight line at a constant velocity (speed). **The same is true of athletes on skis.** But what happens during events like slalom skiing? Athletes have to complete many quick turns while remaining fast and stable. To do this, alpine skiers use their legs to push on the snow against the force of their own momentum—and the more momentum an athlete has, the harder she'll have to push. It isn't unusual for a skier to have to exert hundreds of pounds of force on the snow for several seconds in order to change direction.

So what is momentum, anyway? It's the product of mass (weight) and velocity (speed), and is represented by the following equation:

$$p = mv$$

Where:

- **p = momentum**
- **m = mass**
- **v = velocity**

If you're kind of stumped as to how this is all related, here's one way you can think about it. What's an easier thing to stop: a train moving at 30 miles per hour or a marble moving at 30 miles per hour? If you're a good catch, it's pretty easy to snatch the marble out of the air. But if you tried to grab a moving train, the train would just yank you right along with it! **Why? The train has a lot more mass, meaning it has more momentum than the marble—even if their velocities are the same.**

So what does this mean for skiers? A heavier skier may be able to accelerate faster, because his momentum helps him overcome forces like friction from the snow. Here's the problem, though—in order to turn or come to a full stop, he has to push a whole lot harder on the snow in order to fight against his own momentum!

Try This!

Have a look at the following pairs of moving objects. Which object has the greater momentum? To find out, multiply each object's mass and velocity and pick the larger number.

1. A 7 kg bowling ball traveling at 8 m/s or 0.15 kg baseball traveling at 46 m/s

The bowling ball. 56 kg m/s > 6.9 kg m/s

2. A 92 kg sprinter running at 9 m/s or a 63 kg cyclist on an 11 kg road bike traveling at 12 m/s

The bike + rider. 828 kg m/s < 888 kg m/s

3. A 72 kg alpine snowboarder traveling at 21 m/s or a 61 kg skier traveling at 24 m/s

The alpine snowboarder. 1512 kg m/s > 1464 kg m/s

Winter Olympics
SNOWBOARDING

In the snowboard half-pipe event, snowboarders use velocity and torque to perform tricks in the air.

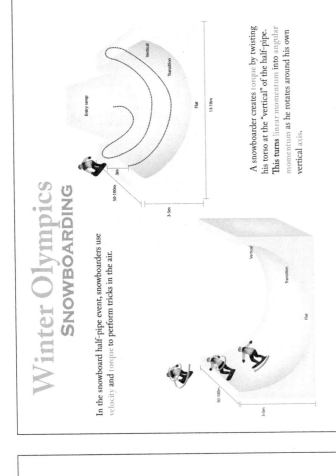

A snowboarder creates torque by twisting his torso at the "vertical" of the half-pipe. This turns linear momentum into angular momentum as he rotates around his own vertical axis.

Try This!

1. Stand up in a clear area. Make sure that you have enough space to reach out both your arms and not touch anything.

2. With your feet about shoulder-width apart, jump straight up. Do this a few times. What kind of momentum is your body experiencing? In what direction?
Your body has linear momentum, in an upward direction (perpendicular to the ground).

3. You're going to jump again, only this time, twist by rotating your chest and shoulders left as you jump. What happened?
When you twisted your chest and shoulders in the air, your whole body rotated left. When you landed, you were facing a different direction from your starting position.

4. Explain how this happened using the terms linear momentum, angular momentum, torque, and axis.
When you jumped and twisted your chest and shoulders, you created torque, which converted your linear momentum into angular momentum and caused you to rotate around your vertical axis.

Winter Olympics
SLALOM SKIING

Check out the illustration above showing a slalom skier during various points of a turn. The red line represents the path that the skier travels in. But remember what Newton's second law says—objects don't naturally travel along curved paths! To complete a turn, a skier has to work hard to change the direction of his momentum (represented by the straight blue lines) by using his legs to exert a force against the snow with the edge of his skis. The force of the snow pushing back on the skis is represented by the green arrow. (This force has a special name. We'll talk about it more when we explore the physics behind speed skating!)

What else do you notice about the diagram above? Do you notice anything the athlete changes about his body positioning throughout the turn? Take note of his hands, torso, and knees. Why do you think he does this?

Explanation: He tucks his arms in front of his body to reduce drag. He leans to the inside of the turn so that he can dig the edges of both skis into the snow, which exerts the frictional force necessary to turn. He bends at the knee on one leg to get into a crouching position, which further reduces drag.

Winter Olympics
SNOWBOARDING

Before a snowboarder does a spin, he extends and "winds up" his arms. By doing this, he's increasing the length of his lever arm, making it easier for his body to rotate. Think about opening a revolving door—is it easier to open by pushing on the edge farthest from the hinge or closer to the hinge? When a snowboarder swings his arms, it increases torque, making it easier for the rest of his body to spin.

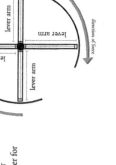

Stand in your original position. Without moving your feet, extend your arms away from your body. Point your right arm in front of you and your left arm behind. Your chest and shoulders should be rotated left. Now, as you jump, swing your arms clockwise. How did **winding up your arms affect your spin?**

Winding up your arms increased the length of the lever arm and created more torque, so it was easier for your body to spin.

_____

Cool Fact:
If snowboarders maximize their torque on the half-pipe, they can spin up to 600° per second—that's nearly two full spins!

Winter Olympics
SHORT TRACK SPEED SKATING

In short track speed skating, competitors race each other around an oval track at speeds of up to 40 miles per hour. How do speed skaters lean so sharply during turns without falling over? **The athlete pictured below isn't supporting any of his weight on his left hand at all!** Remember when we looked at how skiers push on **the snow to turn? The force that pushes back is called** centripetal force because it causes an object to move along a curved path instead of a straight one. Speed skaters turn using this same force, exerted by pushing against the ice with their skates.

Centripetal force leads to an equal and opposite centrifugal force. Centrifugal force comes from inertia—the tendency of an already-moving object to **want to continue moving in a straight line. As the skater turns, he has to work hard to fight against this** tendency. Check out the diagram below:

Need an example of how inertia works? Think about braking really hard in a moving car. Your torso gets "thrown" forward into the seat belt, but this feeling just comes from the fact that your torso wants to keep moving, even though the car is stopping!

Here, we can think of gravity and centrifugal force adding up to one big diagonal force (the dashed green arrow) that pulls on the athlete's center of gravity (g). As long as the athlete uses his skates to push back up through the ice with an equal and opposite force (the blue arrow), he'll remain perfectly balanced during the turn.

Imagine you're riding as a passenger in a car. When the car makes a really sharp turn, why do you feel like you get yanked in the opposite direction? Use the explanation of centrifugal force provided to help you come up with your answer.

Explanation: Your body wants to continue moving straight ahead, but the turning car attempts to pull your body in a new direction. Your body's inertia resists this pull, and you feel this resistance as an apparent force that "throws" you against the inside of the car door!

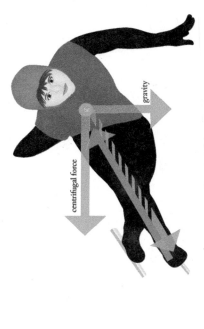

centrifugal force

gravity

Winter Olympics
ICE HOCKEY

Bending the stick against the ice is like compressing a spring. It packs the stick full of **potential energy**. **Hockey sticks, like springs and rubber bands, are elastic objects, which means that they're flexible. When the** hockey stick is in its usual position, which is straight, there's no stored energy. But the hockey stick can be bent some without breaking (this is called **deformation**), but when it's bent, it will try to go back to its normal position. When the stick strikes the puck, that potential energy turns into **kinetic energy**, sending the puck speeding away.

Try This!

1. Get a plastic spoon that can bend about an inch backwards without breaking (biodegradable spoons tend to **be more flexible than other plastic spoons**).

2. Make a tight wad of paper about half an inch in diameter.

3. Hold the spoon from just the handle and load the wad onto the dip in spoon. Fling the spoon forward and observe how the wad travels through the air.

4. Now, do the same thing, only this time, pull back on the top of the spoon so that the handle bends. Release **the spoon and observe how the wad travels through the air. How does this launch compare to the first?** How can you explain this?

Explanation: When you bent the spoon, the wad travelled faster and farther through the air. Bending or deforming the spoon gave it more potential energy, which turned into more kinetic energy after you released the spoon.

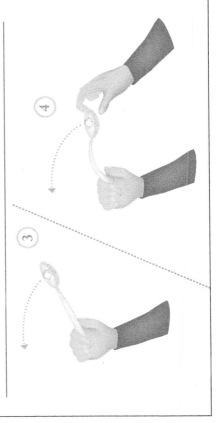

Winter Olympics
SHORT TRACK SPEED SKATING

Try This!

Get a feel for how centripetal and centrifugal forces work! Remember: centripetal force is a push or pull that causes an object to move in a curved path, but because objects have inertia, they resist this pull (remember–moving objects prefer to move in straight lines). We call this resistance centrifugal force.

Procedure

1. Use your permanent marker to mark three evenly spaced points along the edge of your frisbee.

2. Using the hot glue gun, attach one end of each **length of fishing line or string to each marked point** on the frisbee.

3. Place the plastic cup on the center of the frisbee. Don't glue it down.

4. Tie the loose ends of each string together in a knot.

5. Add about 2 inches of water to the cup. You can add a drop of food coloring if you want—this will make it easier to observe the level of the water as you conduct your experiment.

6. Hold the knot you made in step 4 between your **thumb and forefinger.**

7. Swing the apparatus back and forth, slowly increasing the velocity after each swing. Have a friend observe the level of the water. What happens?

8. Try swinging the apparatus so that the string is parallel to the ground. Why doesn't the water spill out? What's responsible for holding the water in the bottom of the cup?

9. **If you're feeling particularly confident, try swinging** the apparatus around in a complete circle. If you do it right, the water shouldn't spill out! How come?

Materials

- **Three 16"lengths of string or fishing line**
- Frisbee
- Hot glue gun
- Plastic cup
- Water
- Food Coloring (optional)
- Permanent marker

Record your observations below, and try to explain the behavior you saw. How can you compare what you observed to how a speed skater keeps his balance during a turn?

_____

_____

_____

_____

(answers will vary)

Winter Olympics
FIGURE SKATING

One of the figure skating moves that makes us "ooh" and "aah" is the spin, where the skater rotates in one spot at a dizzying speed. The skater starts the spin with her arms out, and when she tucks them into her body, she goes even faster.

This is due to the law of conservation of angular momentum. It's harder to make a mass rotate around an axis that's far away than it is to make a mass rotate around an axis that's close. When a skater tucks her arms in, their mass is closer to the axis, so it's easier to rotate—this is called decreasing the moment of inertia. Because angular momentum is conserved, her rotation speed must then increase.

Label the diagram for the variables:
L : angular momentum
I : moment of inertia
ω : angular velocity

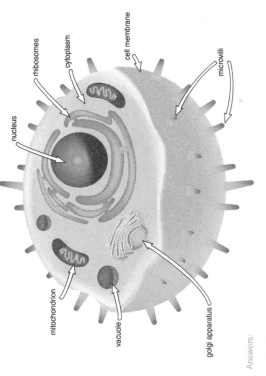

$L = I\omega$

$L = I'\omega'$

I : angular momentum
I : moment of inertia
ω : angular velocity

Try This!

1. Set a swiveling chair in an open room, making sure that while sitting in the chair with your arms and legs extended, you won't hit anything.

2. **Sit in the chair and begin spinning by pushing off the floor with your foot.** Fully extend your arms outward. Keep kicking until you get a good spinning velocity going.

3. **Pull in your arms,** holding them tightly to your chest. What happens? Why?

Explanation: The speed of rotation increases because of the law of conservation of angular momentum. This happens because the mass of your arms is closer to the rotational axis, decreasing the moment of inertia.

4. **Extend your arms outward again.** What happens now? Why?

Explanation: The speed of rotation decreases because the moment of inertia increases as the mass gets farther from the rotational axis.

→ You can repeat the experiment with light weights in your hands, like dumbbells or books, to see an even greater effect!

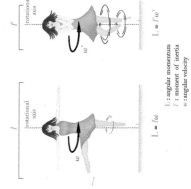

$L = \omega \quad I$

$L = \omega' \quad I'$

Define Cell Parts

Directions: Have an adult help you use a computer to research these parts of a cell. Write what each part of a cell does.

rhibosomes
cytoplasm
nucleus
cell membrane
microvilli
mitochondrion
vacuole
golgi apparatus

Answers:

mitochondrion provides energy for the cell

vacuole contains the waste

golgi apparatus packs protein

nucleus controls the cell

rhibosomes synthesizes (transforms) protein

cytoplasm holds the cell's organelles in place

cell membrane separates the inside of the cell from the outside

microvilli involved in a wide variety of functions, including absorption and secretion

What happens when you eat?

Directions: Color in the different parts of the digestive system, cut them out, and glue them in the right place on the body. (hints: Start at the top. After the tongue, connect the pieces as you go. Glue the small intestines under the large intestines.)

nasal and mouth cavity

stomach

esophagus

small intestines

large intestines

tongue

Brainiac

Directions: Use the clues in the picture to figure out what the different parts of the brain do. Match the part of the brain to the definition.

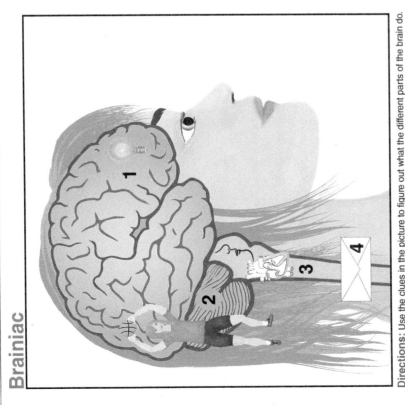

1. cerebrum   a. a bundle of nerves that sends messages to your brain

2. cerebellum   b. the thinking part of the brain

3. brain stem   c. controls balance, movement, and coordination

4. spinal cord   d. keeps you breathing, digesting food, and blood circulating

answers: 1b, 2c, 3d, 4a

Your Respiratory System

Directions: Look at the diagram. Read about what each part of the respiratory system does. Label each part of the respiratory system on the diagram.

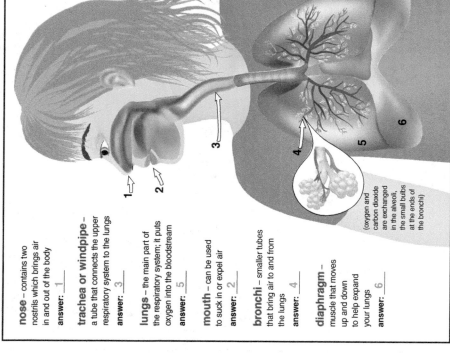

nose – contains two nostrils which brings air in and out of the body

answer: 1

trachea or windpipe – a tube that connects the upper respiratory system to the lungs

answer: 3

lungs – the main part of the respiratory system; it puts oxygen into the bloodstream

answer: 5

mouth – can be used to suck in or expel air

answer: 2

bronchi – smaller tubes that bring air to and from the lungs

answer: 4

diaphragm – muscle that moves up and down to help expand your lungs

answer: 6

(oxygen and carbon dioxide are exchanged in the alveoli, the small bulbs at the ends of the bronchi)

The Body's Filtration System: Kidneys and Intestines

Directions: Cut out each item from the bottom of the page. Each one describes a function of either the kidney or the intestines. Paste each one in the correct column.

	Pushes food through to the anus
Absorbs sodium	
Absorbs potassium	Absorbs nutrients
Absorbs calcium	
Regulates the body's pH balance	Lined with mucus
Cleans out the blood	
The waste from this organ turns into urine	Breaks down food
You can live with only one of these organs	

Pushes food through to the anus	Absorbs potassium	Absorbs nutrients
Regulates the body's pH balance	Cleans out the blood	Absorbs sodium
You can live with only one of these organs	Absorbs calcium	Lined with mucus
The waste from this organ turns into urine		Breaks down food

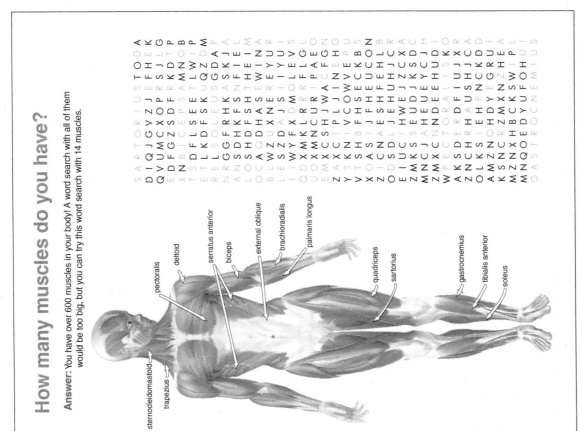

How many muscles do you have?

Answer: You have over 600 muscles in your body! A word search with all of them would be too big, but you can try this word search with 14 muscles.

Labels: sternocleidomastoid, trapezius, pectoralis, deltoid, serratus anterior, biceps, external oblique, brachioradialis, palmaris longus, quadriceps, sartorius, gastrocnemius, tibialis anterior, soleus

```
S A R T O R I U S T O D A
D I Q J G V Z J E F H E K
Q V U M C X O P R S J L G
E D F G Z S D F R K D T P
X N B I C E P S A M N O B
T S D F L S E E T L W I P
E T L K D F S K U Q Z D M
R E L S O L E U S G D A P
N R G G F R H K A S K J A
A N S D H K F S N F I E L
L O C A Q D H A S E W I N A
B L W Z U X N E R E Y U R
L E S Z D A S I Y J U I
Q D X M K L R R F L G L
U O X M N C U R I P A E O
E M X C S H J W A C E H G
Y S K N I V C O W V E P U
V T S H B F H S E C K B S
X Z I C N A E S F H E U C O N
E I U C I H W E J Z C X A
Z M K S S E U D J K S D C
M N C J A H E U E Y C J H
Z M X C N D E E H U D I O
W P E C T O R A L I S K O
A K S D E R D F I U J X R
Z N C H R H A U S H J C A
O L K S I E H P N C K D D
A M Z N O H D Y E G R U I
K S N C R Z M X N Z H E A
M Z N X H B C K S W I P L
M N Q O E D Y U F O H U I
G A S T R O C N E M I U S
```

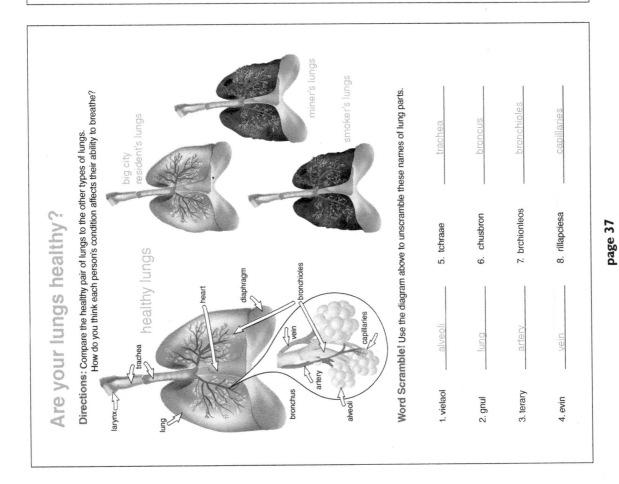

Are your lungs healthy?

Directions: Compare the healthy pair of lungs to the other types of lungs. How do you think each person's condition affects their ability to breathe?

healthy lungs

Labels: larynx, trachea, lung, bronchus, heart, diaphragm, bronchioles, vein, artery, alveoli, capillaries

big city resident's lungs

miner's lungs

smoker's lungs

Word Scramble! Use the diagram above to unscramble these names of lung parts.

1. vielaol ___alveoli___

2. gnul ___lung___

3. terary ___artery___

4. evin ___vein___

5. tchraae ___trachea___

6. chusbron ___broncus___

7. brchionleos ___bronchioles___

8. rillapciesa ___capillaries___

Sorting out the Scientific Method with Dr. E. McSquare

Scientist Dr. E. McSquare is compiling his scientific findings into a single volume. He forgot to give titles to the sections of his reports and now they're all mixed up! Use the definition guide to help Dr. McSquare label his reports.

Definition Guide:

Q = Question: The question is the first part of the scientific process. What question do you want to answer?

H = Hypothesis: A hypothesis is a statement that can be proven true or false. It is often written in the form "If (a) then (b)."

E = Experiment: The experiment is an activity that is used to test if your hypothesis is true or false.

D = Data: Data are the results of the experiment.

C = Conclusion: The conclusion is a final statement that describes what you learned from the experiment and results.

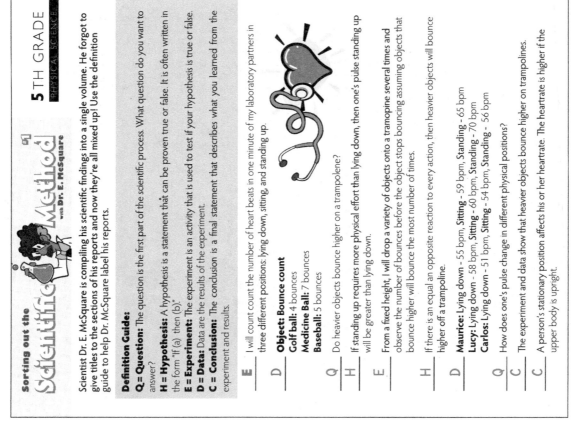

E ___ I will count count the number of heart beats in one minute of my laboratory partners in three different positions: lying down, sitting, and standing up.

D ___ **Object: Bounce count**
Golf ball: 4 bounces
Medicine Ball: 7 bounces
Baseball: 5 bounces

Q ___ Do heavier objects bounce higher on a trampolene?

H ___ If standing up requires more physical effort than lying down, then one's pulse standing up will be greater than lying down.

E ___ From a fixed height, I will drop a variety of objects onto a trampoline several times and observe the number of bounces before the object stops bouncing assuming objects that bounce higher will bounce the most number of times.

H ___ If there is an equal an opposite reaction to every action, then heavier objects will bounce higher off a trampoline.

D ___ **Maurice:** Lying down - 55 bpm, **Sitting** - 59 bpm, **Standing** - 65 bpm
Lucy: Lying down - 58 bpm, **Sitting** - 60 bpm, **Standing** - 70 bpm
Carlos: Lying down - 51 bpm, **Sitting** - 54 bpm, **Standing** - 56 bpm

Q ___ How does one's pulse change in different physical positions?

C ___ The experiment and data show that heavier objects bounce higher on trampolines.

C ___ A person's stationary position affects his or her heartrate. The heartrate is higher if the upper body is upright.

page 48

What does the pancreas do?

Directions: Study the picture, and read the information below. Use the facts to fill in the paragraph below about your pancreas.

The endocrine system is a network of glands that release different hormones to regulate the body. The pancreas is a very unique organ. It is actually a part of two systems, as it does two jobs. The main function is to create hormones like insulin and glucagon.

It also creates digestive enzymes that break down carbohydrates and proteins from foods on the way to the small intestine.

The pancreas is part of the ___endocrine___ system.

There are four main parts of the pancreas:

___head___

___tail___

___body___

and ___pancreatic duct___

The pancreas has ___two___ jobs.

The main job of the pancreas is to release ___hormones___ to regulate the body.

The other job is to create ___digestive enzymes___ that break down carbohydrates and proteins from foods.

The pancreas is a very important part of your body.

page 39

Page 50

Sorting out the
Scientific Method #3
with Dr. E. McSquare

5TH GRADE
PHYSICAL SCIENCE

Scientist Dr. E. McSquare is compiling his scientific findings into a single volume. He forgot to give titles to the sections of his reports and now they're all mixed up! Use the definition guide to help Dr. McSquare label his reports.

Definition Guide:

Q = Question: The question is the first part of the scientific process. What question do you want to answer?

H = Hypothesis: A hypothesis is a statement that can be proven true or false. It is often written in the form "If (a) then (b)."

E = Experiment: The experiment is an activity that is used to test if your hypothesis is true or false.

D = Data: Data are the results of the experiment.

C = Conclusion: The conclusion is a final statement that describes what you learned from the experiment and results.

__H__ If plants reflect green light, then they must absorb red light (the opposite of green) and thus grow more under red lights.

__D__ **Plant Specimen - Light color: Growth**
Yellow Hibiscus - Green light: +9.4cm, Red light: +12.2cm, Blue light: 11.9cm
Golden Sage - Green light: +6.6cm, Red light: +8.1cm, Blue light: +7.1cm
Soybean Plant - Green light: +7.4cm, Red light: +10.1cm, Blue light: +10.0cm
Common Gardenia - Green light: +5.1cm, Red light: +6.9cm, Blue light +6.9cm

__E__ I will place 4 different plant specimen under green lights and compare their growth over the period of a month with identical plants under red and blue lights.

__E__ Using clear containers with measurement marks, I will compare the height of water at room and freezing temperatures.

__Q__ Which color lights cause plants to grow more effectively?

__D__ **Container# - State of water: height**
Container 1 - Water: 14.0ml, ice: 14.8ml
Container 2 - Water: 20.0ml, ice: 20.8ml
Container 3 - Water: 24.0ml, ice: 24.9ml

__Q__ Does water change volume when it freezes?

__C__ After consistent results, water, when frozen, increases in volume in comparison to its liquid form.

__C__ The results of this experiment showed that green light was the least effective color for growing our plants. Blue and red lights caused for the greatest amount of growth to occur.

__H__ If the molecular structure of solids is more dense than liquids, then water will decrease in volume when it freezes.

Page 49

Sorting out the
Scientific Method #2
with Dr. E. McSquare

5TH GRADE
PHYSICAL SCIENCE

Scientist Dr. E. McSquare is compiling his scientific findings into a single volume. He forgot to give titles to the sections of his reports and now they're all mixed up! Use the definition guide to help Dr. McSquare label his reports.

Definition Guide:

Q = Question: The question is the first part of the scientific process. What question do you want to answer?

H = Hypothesis: A hypothesis is a statement that can be proven true or false. It is often written in the form "If (a) then (b)."

E = Experiment: The experiment is an activity that is used to test if your hypothesis is true or false.

D = Data: Data are the results of the experiment.

C = Conclusion: The conclusion is a final statement that describes what you learned from the experiment and results.

__C__ The results of this experiment show that the boiling point of water does rise as the amount of salt in the water increases.

__E__ I will drop a variety of objects from a height of 10 feet and use a stopwatch to record the time it takes for them to hit the ground.

__H__ Ignoring wind resistance, if two objects are dropped at the same time, they will both hit the ground at the same time because gravity is the same for both of them.

__C__ The results of this experiment showed that objects fall at the same rate despite weight differences.

__D__ **Object (weight) (drop time)**
Shoe: (15 oz) (82 seconds)
Bowling ball: (12 pounds) (82 seconds)
Pencil: (2 oz) (84 seconds)

__E__ I will put a thermometer in each of 3 pots of boiling water. Each pot will contain a different amount of salt. I will observe and compare the temperatures in each pot when the water begins to boil.

__Q__ Does adding salt change the temperature at which water begins to boil?

__Q__ Do heavier objects fall faster than lighter objects?

__D__ **Temperature when boiling begins (salt quantity)**
Pot 1: 214.2 F (0g)
Pot 2: 216.3 F (50g)
Pot 3: 218.3 F (100g)

__H__ If adding salt to water increases the density of water, then it requires more energy to make it boil, thus increasing the boiling point temperature.

Hydrogen

Hydrogen is the most common element in the universe. In fact, about 75% of the mass of the universe is made of hydrogen atoms! Hydrogen is the first element on the periodic table and got its name because it is found in water (Hydro means water in Latin). Scientists use the capital letter H to represent Hydrogen.

The chemical formula for water is H_2O. This means there are two hydrogen atoms and one oxygen atom in each water molecule. Look at the chemical formulas below and write how many hydrogen atoms are in each one.

H
1
(1.01)

water H_2O 2

Space ships use hydrogen and oxygen as fuel, the byproduct of the explosion is water.

methane CH_4 4

Methane is a byproduct of decomposing organic matter, it is used as a fuel at some landfills.

glucose $C_6H_{12}O_6$ 12

Glucose is the sugar plants use as food, and is produced through photosynthesis.

ammonia NH_3 3

Ammonia is often used in fertilizers because of its nitrogen content, which is essential for most plants.

caffeine $C_8H_{10}N_4O_2$ 10

Caffeine is found in many plant leaves, it is a natural insecticide because it often kills insects when they ingest it.

vitamin C $C_6H_8O_6$ 8

Vitamin C is important for nearly all animals. Humans are one of only a few species that do not produce it and must get it from food with large amounts of the vitamin.

baking soda $NaHCO_3$ 1

Baking soda is used in the body to neutralize some of the acids produced by the stomach.

Sorting out the

Scientific Method

with Dr. E. McSquare

5TH GRADE
PHYSICAL SCIENCE

Scientist Dr. E. McSquare is compiling his scientific findings into a single volume. He forgot to give titles to the sections of his reports and now they're all mixed up! Use the definition guide to help Dr. McSquare label his reports.

Definition Guide:

Q = Question: The question is the first part of the scientific process. What question do you want to answer?

H = Hypothesis: A hypothesis is a statement that can be proven true or false. It is often written in the form "If (a) then (b)."

E = Experiment: The experiment is an activity that is used to test if your hypothesis is true or false.

D = Data: Data are the results of the experiment.

C = Conclusion: The conclusion is a final statement that describes what you learned from the experiment and results.

Q   Do snails crawl faster on concrete or glass?

D   **Amber: Left eye:** decreased. **Right eye:** decreased.
Julio: Left eye: decreased. **Right eye:** decreased.
Claudia: Left eye: decreased. **Right eye:** decreased.

E   With my laboratory partners, I will cover one eye and shine a light directly into the other. Then, I will categorize the change in pupil size as "increased," "decreased," or "no change."

H   If snails move faster on smoother surfaces, then a snail will move faster on glass than on concrete.

C   The results of the experiment showed that pupil size decreases when there is more light present. This is likely due to the stress direct light causes on the eyes. In order to absorb less light, the pupils shrink.

D   **Snail 1:** Glass - 45s, Concrete - 55s
Snail 2: Glass - 49s, Concrete - 49s
Snail 3: Glass - 55s, Concrete - 56s

H   If a pupil detects the amount of light that is visible, then it will decrease in size when there is more light to take in less light and reduce straining the eye.

C   Snails move faster on glass than on concrete.

Q   What makes the pupil in the eye dilate?

E   I will organize snail races on glass and concrete and compare times of each snail between the surfaces.

Photosynthesis

Use the word bank below to fill in the empty spaces in the paragraph to the right.

Word Bank
CARBON DIOXIDE
CHLOROPHYLL
GLUCOSE
FOOD
LIGHT
BREATHING
WATER

Photosynthesis is a process where plants create their own **food** using sunlight.

Plant leaves absorb red and blue **light** into their leaves, reflecting green light. This is why most plants are green in color. A chemical called **chlorophyll** is found inside most plant cells. This is the substance that absorbs sunlight.

Meanwhile, plants are absorbing **water** (H_2O) through their roots and storing it within their cells. When the sunlight hits the water molecules, the water breaks apart into hydrogen and oxygen.

Plants also take **carbon dioxide** (CO_2) in through holes in their leaves, called stomata. This is a plant's way of **breathing**. When the carbon dioxide combines with hydrogen, a type of sugar called **glucose** is formed. This is a plant's food, and it uses this energy to live and grow. The extra oxygen molecules are released back into the atmosphere.

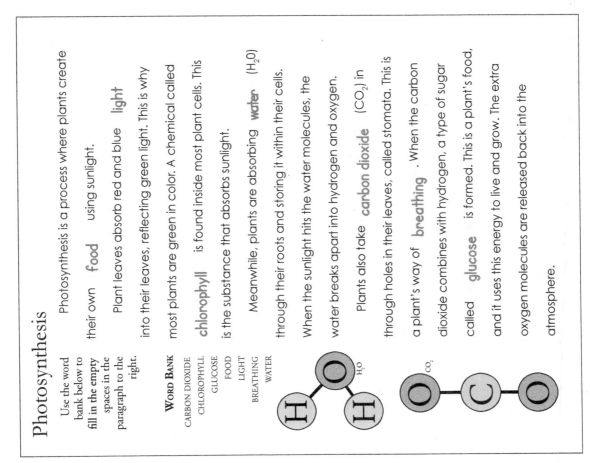

The Water Cycle

Since the beginning of Earth, no water has ever been added to or left our atmosphere. It is constantly moving in a water cycle. Read the definitions below and put the corresponding letter in the squares marking each part of the water cycle in the diagram

A Evaporation:
Liquid water is heated by the sun until it rises as water vapor into the atmosphere.

B Precipitation:
Water falling to the Earth in the form of weather - including rain, sleet, hail and snow.

C Condensation:
Water vapor molecules join together, becoming liquid, in the form of clouds.

D The Sun:
Creates all of the weather on Earth through the uneven heating of Earth's surface.

E Liquid Water:
All living things need this to survive and it is an important part of the weather system.

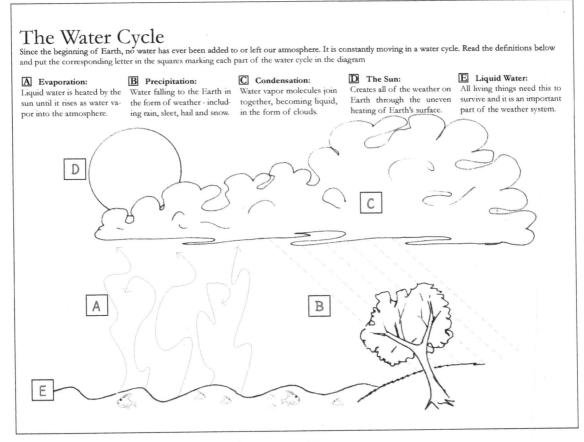

Learn About Tornadoes

A tornado is a spiraling **column** of air that reaches from a cloud to land. Tornadoes can reach speeds of up to **300** miles per hour and can cause significant destruction! In the **U.S.A.** there are about 1,000 tornadoes each year. Most of these tornadoes occur in an area called Tornado Alley. Tornado Alley is right in the middle of the country and includes the states Texas, Kansas and **Oklahoma**.

Most tornadoes form during **thunderstorms**. When warm, moist air and cool, dry air mix the atmosphere becomes unstable. With a change in wind speed and direction a spinning effect begins to take place.

Rising air within this **updraft** tilts the rotating air into a vertical position. This column of rotating air is usually between two and six miles wide. **funnel** clouds can form within this area. When a funnel cloud reaches the **ground** it is called a tornado.

Use the word bank **below to fill in the** empty spaces in the paragraph.

WORD BANK

300
GROUND
THUNDERSTORMS
UPDRAFT
FUNNEL
COLUMN
U.S.A.
OKLAHOMA

The Sun

What is the difference between a flare and a prominence?

A flare flashes off of the sun's surface, while a prominence loops back to the sun's surface

What part of the sun produces the majority of heat and light?

The core produces the majority of the sun's heat and light

What two parts of the sun's outer layer are only visible from Earth during a solar eclipse?

The corona and the chromosphere are both visible during a solar eclipse, but normally are not visible to the naked eye

Why are sunspots darker than surrounding areas?

Sunspots are darker than surrounding areas because they are a lower temperature

What part of the sun do we see from Earth?

We can see the photosphere from Earth

Learn About Hurricanes

Use the word bank to fill the empty spaces in the paragraph.

WORD BANK

ISLANDS
HUMID
OCEAN
ENERGY
RAIN
MILES
WINDS
SPIRALS

A hurricane is a huge storm that forms over the open **ocean**. Hurricanes are made up of strong **winds** and are usually accompanied by heavy **rain**. They can create large waves and cause a great amount of damage. Because a hurricane only travels over open ocean waters the places most at risk are **islands** and coastal towns. Hurricanes are formed over ocean water that is 80° F or warmer. The warm water provides **energy** for the hurricane. Winds come together above the water and force the air upward. **Humid** air, which is hot and moist, rises from the water to create storm-clouds. Above the storm clouds wind flows outward and allows the air to rise. The wind **spirals** around and around the storm. This storm becomes a hurricane when the cyclone reaches wind speeds of at least 74 **miles** per hour.

page 58

Pollination is very important and neccessary to the reproduction of plants. There are several stems within a flower. These are called **stamen**. At the top of each stamen is a small pad where **pollen** sits. At the center of a flower there is a tube. The top of the tube is a sticky platform called a **stigma**. Pollen from the stamen must be transported to the stigma. This is typically done when bees and other insects feed on the nectar of the flower. The pollen sticks to the feeding bee. When the bee flies away to feed on another flower, it carries the pollen from the first flower to the stigma of the second flower. From the stigma pollen travels through a tube called the **pistil** down to the base of the flower. At the base of the flower is the **ovule**. That is where the pollen mixes with the other reproductive elements of the flower to make the seeds for new plants. It is important that the pollen of one flower reaches the stigma of the other. This creates diversity in the new plant's genes. Diversity means the new plant will not not inherit all the traits of either of its parents so it is less likely to inherit any problems they might have had.

First, find the different parts of the flower in the diagram, label and color them in. Color the stamen black, the pollen yellow, the stigma red, the pistil green and the ovule blue. Then with a blue line trace the path the bee must take to pollinate these two flowers. Using a green line trace the path the pollen takes to create new seeds with a different plant.

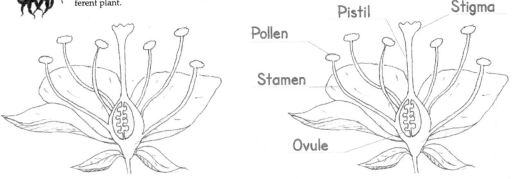

page 60

113

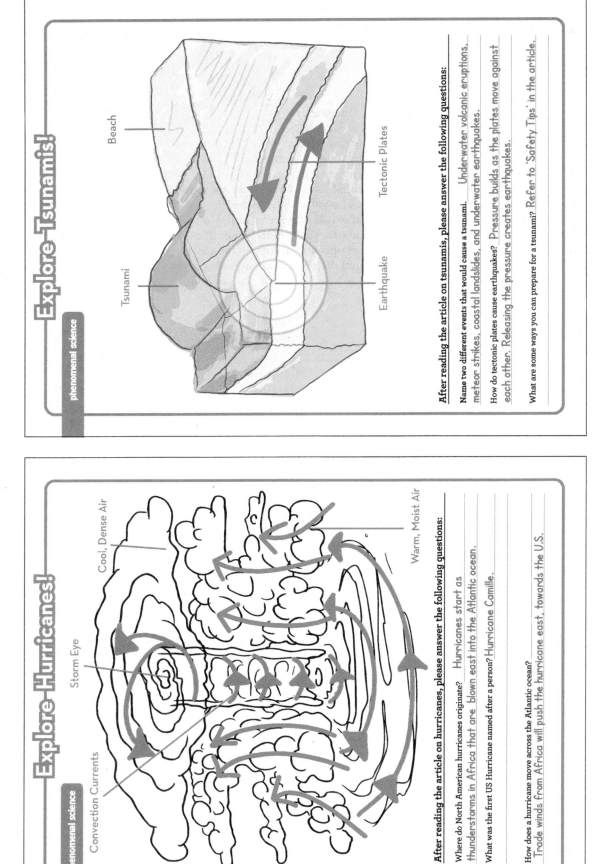

Explore Tsunamis!

phenomenal science

Beach

Tsunami

Tectonic Plates

Earthquake

After reading the article on tsunamis, please answer the following questions:

Name two different events that would cause a tsunami. Underwater volcanic eruptions, meteor strikes, coastal landslides, and underwater earthquakes.

How do tectonic plates cause earthquakes? Pressure builds as the plates move against each other. Releasing the pressure creates earthquakes.

What are some ways you can prepare for a tsunami? Refer to 'Safety Tips' in the article.

page 65

Explore Hurricanes!

phenomenal science

Cool, Dense Air

Storm Eye

Convection Currents

Warm, Moist Air

After reading the article on hurricanes, please answer the following questions:

Where do North American hurricanes originate? Hurricanes start as thunderstorms in Africa that are blown east into the Atlantic ocean.

What was the first US Hurricane named after a person? Hurricane Camille.

How does a hurricane move across the Atlantic ocean? Trade winds from Africa will push the hurricane east, towards the U.S.

page 63

Explore Tornadoes!

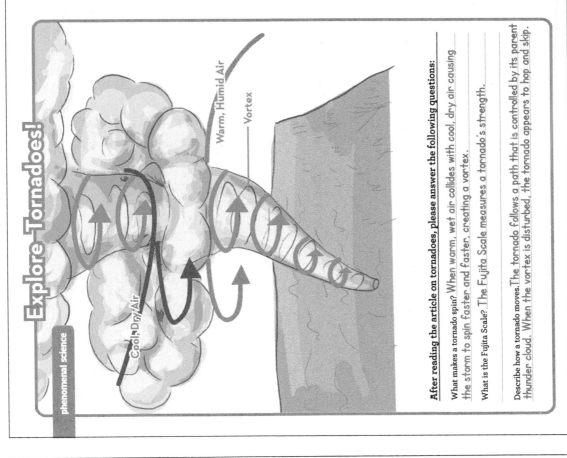

Cool, Dry Air

Warm, Humid Air

Vortex

After reading the article on tornadoes, please answer the following questions:

What makes a tornado spin? When warm, wet air collides with cool, dry air causing the storm to spin faster and faster, creating a vortex.

What is the Fujita Scale? The Fujita Scale measures a tornado's strength.

Describe how a tornado moves. The tornado follows a path that is controlled by its parent thunder cloud. When the vortex is disturbed, the tornado appears to hop and skip.

page 69

Explore Earthquakes!

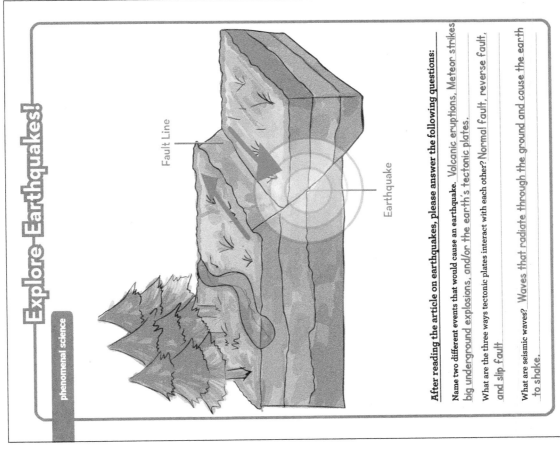

Fault Line

Earthquake

After reading the article on earthquakes, please answer the following questions:

Name two different events that would cause an earthquake. Volcanic eruptions. Meteor strikes, big underground explosions, and/or the earth's tectonic plates.

What are the three ways tectonic plates interact with each other? Normal fault, reverse fault, and slip fault

What are seismic waves? Waves that radiate through the ground and cause the earth to shake.

page 67

Speed of Light

In outer space, where there are no air particles, the speed of light is 299,792,458 meters per second. That is approximately 186,000 miles per second!

DID YOU KNOW

The starlight we see in the night sky is actually tens to hundreds of years old! Although their light travels very fast across the vacuum of space, the stars are so far away that their light takes many years to reach Earth. Light travels much faster than sound.

In fact, the sun's light takes 8 minutes to reach us on Earth. In theory, if the sun were to go out, we wouldn't know until 8 minutes after it happened.

The length of time it takes light to go from:

Moon to Earth:
1.2 seconds

Earth to Sun:
8.5 seconds

THINK ABOUT IT:

Why do we count the seconds in between the lighting flash and the sound of the thunder?

The flash of light and the sound of thunder are both caused by a lighting bolt. But since sound only travels about 1/5 of a mile every second, it takes much longer for the sound of thunder to reach our ears than the flash of light takes to reach our eyes. You can actually estimate how far away a lightning strike is by counting the difference in seconds between the flash and the sound of thunder!

Speed of Sound

Sound travels at different speeds, depending on how fast the vibrations are passed from particle to particle. Because of this, sound travels at different speeds through different materials.

A)

MATERIAL	SPEED OF SOUND
Rubber	60 meters/second
Air	340 meters/second
Lead	1210 meters/second
Glass	4540 meters/second
Aluminum	6320 meters/second

B)

SPEED OF SOUND

Sound Waves

THINK ABOUT IT! (Use chart A for the following questions)

Why does sound travel at different speeds through different materials?

All materials are made of different particles, and some particles vibrate the sound faster (or slower) than others.

In chart A, what material does sound move through the fastest? Why do you think this happens?

Aluminum moves sound fastest, because it is the least dense of the materials on the list. It vibrates sound very quickly.

CHALLENGE QUESTION

If a sound wave travels through the air a approximately 750 miles per hour, how many seconds does it take for that sound wave to travel one mile?

Hint: Speed = Distance ÷ Time

First find miles per second.   To do that, find the number of seconds in 1 hour.
60 x 60 = 3,600 seconds in one hour.

Then, calculate how many miles per second it travels 750 / 3,600 = .21
≈ .20 miles per second = 1/5 mps

The sound wave travels 1/5 of a mile per second, so it takes
5 seconds to go 1 mile!

DID YOU KNOW?

Researchers who looked at results from the 2004 Olympics say sprinters who were closest to the gun took off faster, probably because they perceived the shot faster and louder than their competitors did.

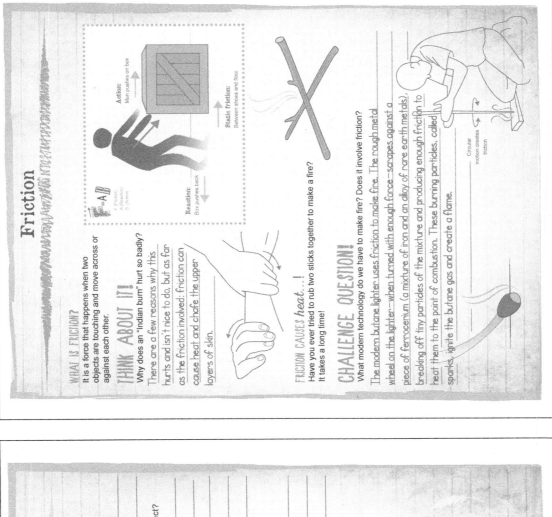

Friction

WHAT IS FRICTION?
It is a force that happens when two objects are touching and move across or against each other.

THINK ABOUT IT!
Why does an "Indian burn" hurt so badly?
There are a few reasons why this hurts and isn't nice to do, but as far as the friction involved: friction can cause heat and chafe the upper layers of skin.

FRICTION CAUSES heat...!
Have you ever tried to rub two sticks together to make a fire? It takes a long time!

CHALLENGE QUESTION!
What modern technology do we have to make fire? Does it involve friction?

The modern butane lighter uses friction to make fire. The rough metal wheel on the lighter—when turned with enough force—scrapes against a piece of ferrocerium (a mixture of iron and an alloy of rare earth metals), breaking off tiny particles of the mixture and producing enough friction to heat them to the point of combustion. These burning particles, called sparks, ignite the butane gas and create a flame.

Action: Man pushes on box

$F = A \cdot B$
F (Friction)
A (Reaction)
B (Action)

Reaction: Box pushes back

Static friction: Between shoes and floor

Circular motion creates friction

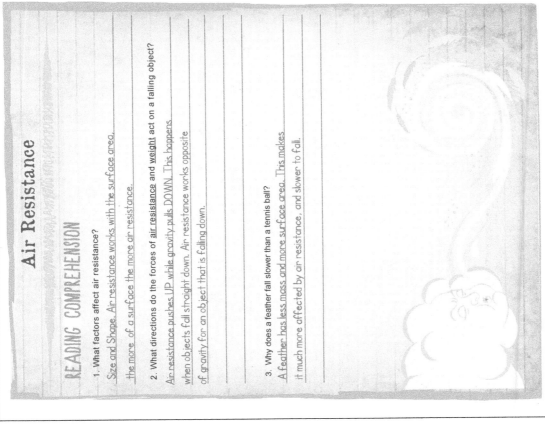

Air Resistance

READING COMPREHENSION

1. What factors affect air resistance?

Size and Shape. Air resistance works with the surface area, the more of a surface the more air resistance.

2. What directions do the forces of air resistance and weight act on a falling object?

Air resistance pushes UP while gravity pulls DOWN. This happens when objects fall straight down. Air resistance works opposite of gravity for an object that is falling down.

3. Why does a feather fall slower than a tennis ball?

A feather has less mass and more surface area. This makes it much more affected by air resistance, and slower to fall.

Newton's First Law — The Law of Inertia

THE LAW OF INERTIA
An object at rest will remain at rest unless acted on by an unbalanced force. An object in motion continues in motion with the same speed and in the same direction unless acted upon by an unbalanced force.

THINK ABOUT IT!

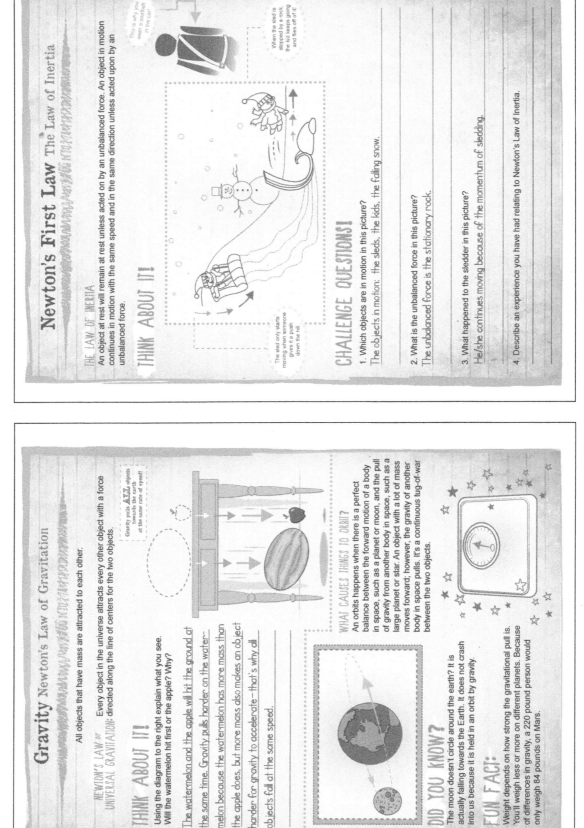

This is why you wear a seatbelt in the car!

When the sled is stopped by a rock, the kid keeps going and flies off of it!

The sled only starts moving when someone gives it a push down the hill

CHALLENGE QUESTIONS!

1. Which objects are in motion in this picture?
The objects in motion: the sleds, the kids, the falling snow.

2. What is the unbalanced force in this picture?
The unbalanced force is the stationary rock.

3. What happened to the sledder in this picture?
He/she continues moving because of the momentum of sledding.

4. Describe an experience you have had relating to Newton's Law of Inertia.

Gravity — Newton's Law of Gravitation

NEWTON'S LAW OF UNIVERSAL GRAVITATION: Every object in the universe attracts every other object with a force directed along the line of centers for the two objects.

All objects that have mass are attracted to each other.

THINK ABOUT IT!
Using the diagram to the right explain what you see.
Will the watermelon hit first or the apple? Why?

The watermelon and the apple will hit the ground at the same time. Gravity pulls harder on the watermelon because the watermelon has more mass than the apple does, but more mass also makes an object harder for gravity to accelerate—that's why all objects fall at the same speed.

Gravity pulls ALL objects towards the earth at the same rate of speed!

WHAT CAUSES THINGS TO ORBIT?
An orbit happens when there is a perfect balance between the forward motion of a body in space, such as a planet or moon, and the pull of gravity from another body in space, such as a large planet or star. An object with a lot of mass moves forward; however, the gravity of another body in space pulls. It's a continuous tug-of-war between the two objects.

DID YOU KNOW?
The moon doesn't circle around the earth? It is actually falling towards the Earth. It does not crash into us because it is held in an orbit by gravity.

FUN FACT:
Weight depends on how strong the gravitational pull is. You'll weigh less or more on different planets. Because of differences in gravity, a 220 pound person would only weigh 84 pounds on Mars.

Newton's Law The Action-Reaction Law

1. Trick Question:

The force exerted by the car is the same as the force exerted by the bug, because for every action there is an equal and opposite reaction! The fact that the bug splatters only means that with its smaller mass, it is less able to handle the acceleration of the larger mass (the car) resulting from the impact.

2. C. The force of the rifle equals the force of the bullet.

Newton's Second Law The Law of Acceleration

ACCELERATION is produced when a force acts on a mass. The greater the mass of the object being accelerated, the greater amount of force needed to accelerate the object.

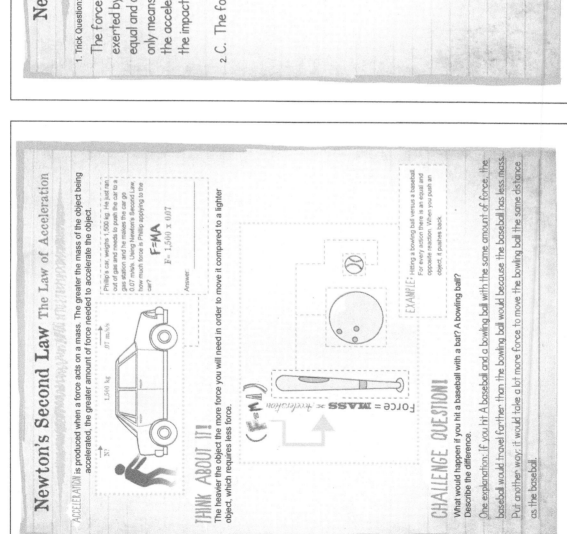

1,500 kg   N?   .07 m/s/s

Phillip's car, weighs 1,500 kg. He just ran out of gas and needs to push the car to a gas station and he makes the car go 0.07 m/s/s. Using Newton's Second Law, how much force is Phillip applying to the car?

$$F=MA$$
$$F = 1,500 \times 0.07$$

Answer: _____

THINK ABOUT IT!

The heavier the object the more force you will need in order to move it compared to a lighter object, which requires less force.

$$(F=MA)$$

FORCE = MASS × Acceleration

CHALLENGE QUESTION!

What would happen if you hit a baseball with a bat? A bowling ball? Describe the difference.

One explanation: If you hit A baseball and a bowling ball with the same amount of force, the baseball would travel farther than the bowling ball would because the baseball has less mass. Put another way: it would take a lot more force to move the bowling ball the same distance as the baseball.

EXAMPLE: Hitting a bowling ball versus a baseball. For every action there is an equal and opposite reaction. When you push an object, it pushes back

Energy

E = mc²

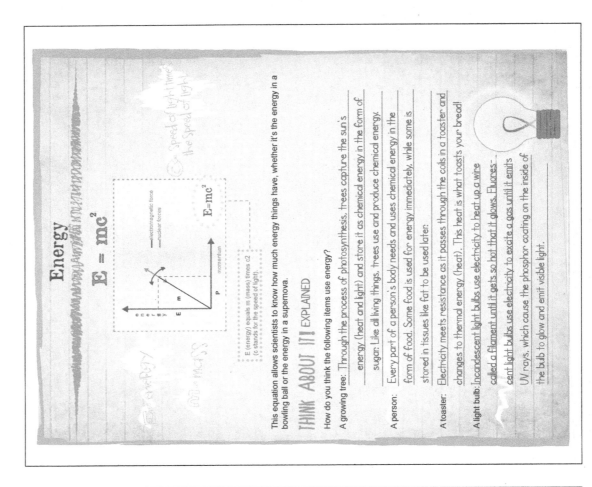

- E (energy) equals m (mass) times c2 (c stands for the speed of light).

E=mc²

Speed of light times the speed of light

This equation allows scientists to know how much energy things have, whether it's the energy in a bowling ball or the energy in a supernova.

THINK ABOUT IT! EXPLAINED

How do you think the following items use energy?

A growing tree: Through the process of photosynthesis, trees capture the sun's energy (heat and light) and store it as chemical energy in the form of sugar. Like all living things, trees use and produce chemical energy.

A person: Every part of a person's body needs and uses chemical energy in the form of food. Some food is used for energy immediately, while some is stored in tissues like fat to be used later.

A toaster: Electricity meets resistance as it passes through the coils in a toaster and changes to thermal energy (heat). This heat is what toasts your bread!

A light bulb: Incandescent light bulbs use electricity to heat up a wire called a filament until it gets so hot that it glows. Fluorescent light bulbs use electricity to excite a gas until it emits UV rays, which cause the phosphor coating on the inside of the bulb to glow and emit visible light.

What is Energy?

MATCH THE ENERGY!

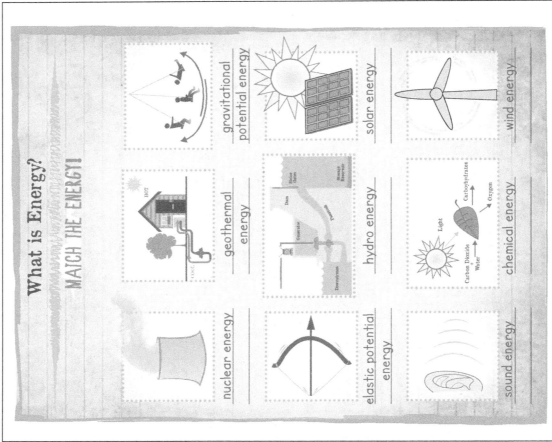

gravitational potential energy

geothermal energy

nuclear energy

solar energy

hydro energy

elastic potential energy

wind energy

chemical energy

sound energy

Condensation and Evaporation

CHALLENGE QUESTION:

1. Hanging Wet Clothes
Where do you think would be the best place to put your clothes/materials so that they will dry as quickly as possible? Draw a picture showing what you think will happen to the water.

Answers will vary.

One idea: Hanging clothes up in a dry area would help with faster drying. Outside where airflow, and possibly heat from the sun, is present could be one place to hang clothes.

2. Condensation of Breath in Air
Describe what you think is happening when you can see your breath in the air. Where do you think it comes from? Do you think you can make it go away? A brief explanation:

There is moisture in our breath, because our lungs, mouth, and airway is moist. It's also warm inside our lungs. When we exhale, water vapor (water in gas form) comes out, too. When it's cold outside the water vapor in an exhaled breath cools and condenses into drops of liquid water that can be seen in the air; like fog. When it's warm outside we don't see our breath because the air is warm enough to let the water vapor remain a gas.

The Physics of Lightning

What is happening when lightning strikes the ground?

Cloud

As the NEGATIVE charges collect at the bottom of the cloud it forces the negative charges in the ground to be forced away from the surface. This leaves the ground POSITIVE.

As the negative charges approach the ground, a stream of positive charges repelled by the ground attract to the negative stream.

When connected they have created path which allows a sudden down surge of electrons to jump to the ground

This is the lightning.

Earth

DID YOU KNOW?

Cars are a very safe place to be, and it's not the rubber tires that protect you! This is a very common misconception. It is actually the metal that is surrounding you that acts like a cage of protection. This is due to the Skin Effect which says that electricity, like lightning, will travel only on the surface of enclosed metal objects. So while your car may be hit by lightning, if you stay inside you will be safe.

CHALLENGE QUESTION: Why are you safer if you are lower to the ground?

Lightning is charged ions. Trying to cancel their charge by connecting with the ground, taking the shortest path, staying as low as possible is the best idea. The ground is hit by lightning often enough, but trees get struck more often.

Super Hero Physics!

Now that you have learned all about physics, if you were a *Super Hero*, what would your powers be?

Answers may vary.

Would you rather be able to move at the speed of sound or the speed of light?

Speed of light! It is much faster than the speed of sound.

Who is Sound Man's arch nemesis?

Vacuum Man... Outer Space Man... etc.

If you had the gift of super friction, what would you be able to do?

Walk on walls, run really fast, create fire with your fingertips, etc.

Lightning Boy is about to strike! Where will you hide?

In a car, close to the ground ... etc.

Who does better in the water:
Sound Man or Light Man? What about in outer space?

Sound Man goes faster in the water, and

Light Man goes faster in outer space.

What special features does Air Resistance Man's super suit have?

Air Resistance Man's suit will probably not be

affected by Air Resistance; or perhaps it has

the power to manipulate air molecules to slow

down his opponents.

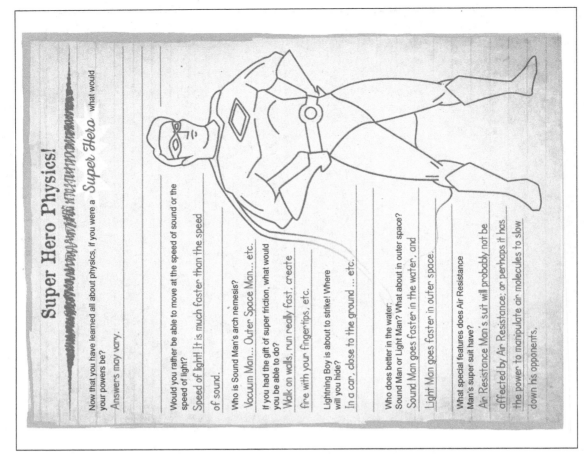

Magnet Myths

1. If you can manipulate metal to be magnetic, do you think you can demagnetize something? How would this work?

You can reduce the strength of a magnet (or completely demagnetize it) by exposing it to a magnetic field that is aligned in the opposite direction.

2. Magnets do one of two things, repel or attract. Why is this?

There are two types of electric charges, positive and negative, or north and south pole. If the same pole of two magnets are put close to each other they will repel, or push apart. If different poles are close to each other, they will be attracted to each other and pull together.